John Griffith London (born **John Griffith Chaney**; January 12, 1876 – November 22, 1916) was an American novelist, journalist, and social activist. A pioneer in the world of commercial magazine fiction, he was one of the first writers to become a worldwide celebrity and earn a large fortune from writing. He was also an innovator in the genre that would later become known as science fiction. His most famous works include The Call of the Wild and White Fang, both set in the Klondike Gold Rush, as well as the short stories "To Build a Fire", "An Odyssey of the North", and "Love of Life". He also wrote about the South Pacific in stories such as "The Pearls of Parlay" and "The Heathen". London was part of the radical literary group "The Crowd" in San Francisco and a passionate advocate of unionization, socialism, and the rights of workers. He wrote several powerful works dealing with these topics, such as his dystopian novel The Iron Heel, his non-fiction exposé The People of the Abyss, and The War of the Classes. (Source: Wikipedia)

Literary works:
The Cruise of the Dazzler (1902)
A Daughter of the Snows (1902)
The Call of the Wild (1903)
The Kempton-Wace Letters (1903)
The Sea-Wolf (1904)
The Game (1905)
White Fang (1906)
Before Adam (1907)
The Iron Heel (1908)
Martin Eden (1909)
Burning Daylight (1910)
Adventure (1911)
The Scarlet Plague (1912)
A Son of the Sun (1912)
The Abysmal Brute (1913)
The Valley of the Moon (1913)

DUTCH COURAGE
AND
OTHER STORIES
JACK LONDON

PRINCE CLASSICS

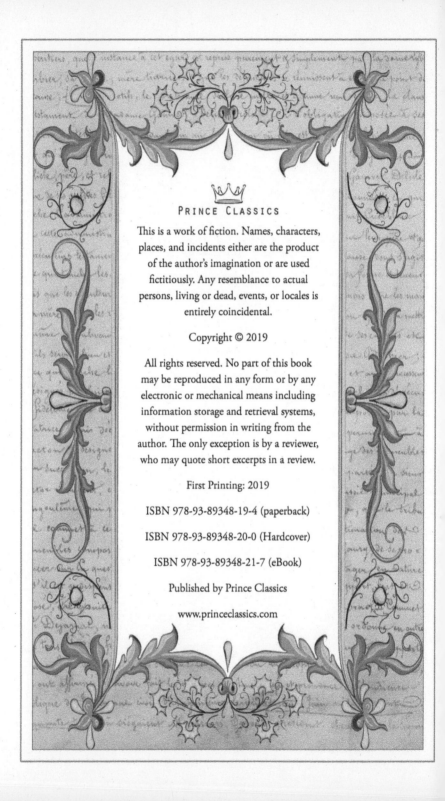

PRINCE CLASSICS

First Printing: 2019

ISBN 978-93-89348-19-4 (paperback)

ISBN 978-93-89348-20-0 (Hardcover)

ISBN 978-93-89348-21-7 (eBook)

Published by Prince Classics

www.princeclassics.com

Contents

DUTCH COURAGE
AND
OTHER STORIES

PREFACE

"I've never written a line that I'd be ashamed for my young daughters to read, and I never shall write such a line!"

Thus Jack London, well along in his career. And thus almost any collection of his adventure stories is acceptable to young readers as well as to their elders. So, in sorting over the few manuscripts still unpublished in book form, while most of them were written primarily for boys and girls, I do not hesitate to include as appropriate a tale such as "Whose Business Is to Live."

Number two of the present group, "Typhoon Off the Coast of Japan," is the first story ever written by Jack London for publication. At the age of seventeen he had returned from his deep-water voyage in the sealing schooner Sophie Sutherland, and was working thirteen hours a day for forty dollars a month in an Oakland, California, jute mill. The San Francisco Call offered a prize of twenty-five dollars for the best written descriptive article. Jack's mother, Flora London, remembering that I had excelled in his school "compositions," urged him to enter the contest by recalling some happening of his travels. Grammar school, years earlier, had been his sole disciplined education. But his wide reading, worldly experience, and extraordinary powers of observation and correlation, enabled him to command first prize. It is notable that the second and third awards went to students at California and Stanford universities.

Jack never took the trouble to hunt up that old San Francisco Call of November 12, 1893; but when I came to write his biography, "The Book of Jack London," I unearthed the issue, and the tale appears intact in my English edition, published in 1921. And now, gathering material for what will be the final Jack London collections, I cannot but think that his first printed story will have unusual interest for his readers of all ages.

The boy Jack's unexpected success in that virgin venture naturally spurred him to further effort. It was, for one thing, the pleasantest way he had ever earned so much money, even if it lacked the element of physical prowess and danger that had marked those purple days with the oyster pirates, and, later, equally exciting passages with the Fish Patrol. He only waited to catch up on sleep lost while hammering out "Typhoon Off the Coast of Japan," before applying himself to new fiction. That was what was the matter with it: it was sheer fiction in place of the white-hot realism of the "true story" that had brought him distinction. This second venture he afterward termed "gush." It was promptly rejected by the editor of the Call. Lacking experience in such matters, Jack could not know why. And it did not occur to him to submit his manuscript elsewhere. His fire was dampened; he gave over writing and continued with the jute mill and innocent social diversion in company with Louis Shattuck and his friends, who had superseded Jack's wilder comrades and hazards of bay- and sea-faring. This period, following the publication of "Typhoon Off the Coast of Japan," is touched upon in his book "John Barleycorn."

The next that one hears of attempts at writing is when, during his tramping episode, he showed some stories to his aunt, Mrs. Everhard, in St. Joseph, Michigan. And in the ensuing months of that year, 1894, she received other romances mailed at his stopping places along the eastward route, alone or with Kelly's Industrial Army. As yet it had not sunk into his consciousness that his unyouthful knowledge of life in the raw would be the means of success in literature; therefore he discoursed of imaginary things and persons, lords and ladies, days of chivalry and what not—anything but out of his priceless first-hand lore. At the same time, however, he kept a small diary which, in the days when he had found himself, helped in visualizing his tramp life, in "The Road."

The only out and out "juvenile" in the Jack London list prior to his death is "The Cruise of the Dazzler," published in 1902. At that it is a good and authentic maritime study of its kind, and not lacking in honest thrills. "Tales of the Fish Patrol" comes next as a book for boys; but the happenings told therein are perilous enough to interest many an older reader.

I am often asked which of his books have made the strongest appeal to youth. The impulse is to answer that it depends upon the particular type of youth. As example, there lies before me a letter from a friend: "Ruth (she is eleven) has been reading every book of your husband's that she can get hold of. She is crazy over the stories. I have bought nearly all of them, but cannot find 'The Son of the Wolf,' 'Moon Face,' and 'Michael Brother of Jerry.' Will you tell me where I can order these?" I have not yet learned Ruth's favorites; but I smile to myself at thought of the re-reading she may have to do when her mind has more fully developed.

The youth of every country who read Jack London naturally turn to his adventure stories—particularly "The Call of the Wild" and its companion "White Fang," "The Sea Wolf," "The Cruise of the Snark," and my own journal, "The Log of the Snark," and "Our Hawaii," "Smoke Bellew Tales," "Adventure," "The Mutiny of the Elsinore," as well as "Before Adam," "The Game," "The Abysmal Brute," "The Road," "Jerry of the Islands" and its sequel "Michael Brother of Jerry." And because of the last named, the youth of many lands are enrolling in the famous Jack London Club. This was inspired by Dr. Francis H. Bowley, President of the Massachusetts S.P.C.A. The Club expects no dues. Membership is automatic through the mere promise to leave any playhouse during an animal performance. The protest thereby registered is bound, in good time, to do away with the abuses that attend animal training for show purposes. "Michael Brother of Jerry" was written out of Jack London's heart of love and head of understanding of animals, aided by a years'-long study of the conditions of which he treats. Incidentally this book contains one of the most charming bits of seafaring romance of the Southern Ocean that he ever wrote.

During the Great War, the English speaking soldiers called freely for the foregoing novels, dubbing them "The Jacklondons"; and there was also lively demand for "Burning Daylight," "The Scarlet Plague," "The Star Rover," "The Little Lady of the Big House," "The Valley of the Moon," and, because of its prophetic spirit, "The Iron Heel." There was likewise a desire for the short-story collections, such as "The God of His Fathers," "Children of the Frost," "The Faith of Men," "Love of Life," "Lost Face," "When God Laughs," and later groups like "South Sea Tales," "A Son of the Sun," "The Night Born," and "The House of Pride," and a long list beside.

But for the serious minded youth of America, Great Britain, and all countries where Jack London's work has been translated—youth considering life with a purpose—"Martin Eden" is the beacon. Passing years only augment the number of messages that find their way to me from near and far, attesting the worth to thoughtful boys and girls, young men and women, of the author's own formative struggle in life and letters as partially outlined in "Martin Eden."

The present sheaf of young folk's stories were written during the latter part of that battle for recognition, and my gathering of them inside book covers is pursuant of his own intention at the time of his death on November 22, 1916.

CHARMIAN LONDON.

Jack London Ranch,

Glen Ellen, Sonoma County, California.

August 1, 1922.

DUTCH COURAGE

"Just our luck!"

Gus Lafee finished wiping his hands and sullenly threw the towel upon the rocks. His attitude was one of deep dejection. The light seemed gone out of the day and the glory from the golden sun. Even the keen mountain air was devoid of relish, and the early morning no longer yielded its customary zest.

"Just our luck!" Gus repeated, this time avowedly for the edification of another young fellow who was busily engaged in sousing his head in the water of the lake.

"What are you grumbling about, anyway?" Hazard Van Dorn lifted a soap-rimmed face questioningly. His eyes were shut. "What's our luck?"

"Look there!" Gus threw a moody glance skyward. "Some duffer's got ahead of us. We've been scooped, that's all!"

Hazard opened his eyes, and caught a fleeting glimpse of a white flag waving arrogantly on the edge of a wall of rock nearly a mile above his head. Then his eyes closed with a snap, and his face wrinkled spasmodically. Gus threw him the towel, and uncommiseratingly watched him wipe out the offending soap. He felt too blue himself to take stock in trivialities.

Hazard groaned.

"Does it hurt—much?" Gus queried, coldly, without interest, as if it were no more than his duty to ask after the welfare of his comrade.

"I guess it does," responded the suffering one.

"Soap's pretty strong, eh?—Noticed it myself."

"'Tisn't the soap. It's—it's that!" He opened his reddened eyes and pointed toward the innocent white little flag. "That's what hurts."

Gus Lafee did not reply, but turned away to start the fire and begin cooking breakfast. His disappointment and grief were too deep for anything but silence, and Hazard, who felt likewise, never opened his mouth as he fed the horses, nor once laid his head against their arching necks or passed caressing fingers through their manes. The two boys were blind, also, to the manifold glories of Mirror Lake which reposed at their very feet. Nine times, had they chosen to move along its margin the short distance of a hundred yards, could they have seen the sunrise repeated; nine times, from behind as many successive peaks, could they have seen the great orb rear his blazing rim; and nine times, had they but looked into the waters of the lake, could they have seen the phenomena reflected faithfully and vividly. But all the Titanic grandeur of the scene was lost to them. They had been robbed of the chief pleasure of their trip to Yosemite Valley. They had been frustrated in their long-cherished design upon Half Dome, and hence were rendered disconsolate and blind to the beauties and the wonders of the place.

Half Dome rears its ice-scarred head fully five thousand feet above the level floor of Yosemite Valley. In the name itself of this great rock lies an accurate and complete description. Nothing more nor less is it than a cyclopean, rounded dome, split in half as cleanly as an apple that is divided by a knife. It is, perhaps, quite needless to state that but one-half remains, hence its name, the other half having been carried away by the great ice-river in the stormy time of the Glacial Period. In that dim day one of those frigid rivers gouged a mighty channel from out the solid rock. This channel to-day is Yosemite Valley. But to return to the Half Dome. On its northeastern side, by circuitous trails and stiff climbing, one may gain the Saddle. Against the slope of the Dome the Saddle leans like a gigantic slab, and from the top of this slab, one thousand feet in length, curves the great circle to the summit of the Dome. A few degrees too steep for unaided climbing, these one thousand feet defied for years the adventurous spirits who fixed yearning eyes upon the crest above.

One day, a couple of clear-headed mountaineers had proceeded to insert iron eye-bolts into holes which they drilled into the rock every few feet apart. But when they found themselves three hundred feet above the Saddle, clinging like flies to the precarious wall with on either hand a yawning abyss, their nerves failed them and they abandoned the enterprise. So it remained for an indomitable Scotchman, one George Anderson, finally to achieve the feat. Beginning where they had left off, drilling and climbing for a week, he had at last set foot upon that awful summit and gazed down into the depths where Mirror Lake reposed, nearly a mile beneath.

In the years which followed, many bold men took advantage of the huge rope ladder which he had put in place; but one winter ladder, cables and all were carried away by the snow and ice. True, most of the eye-bolts, twisted and bent, remained. But few men had since essayed the hazardous undertaking, and of those few more than one gave up his life on the treacherous heights, and not one succeeded.

But Gus Lafee and Hazard Van Dorn had left the smiling valley-land of California and journeyed into the high Sierras, intent on the great adventure. And thus it was that their disappointment was deep and grievous when they awoke on this morning to receive the forestalling message of the little white flag.

"Camped at the foot of the Saddle last night and went up at the first peep of day," Hazard ventured, long after the silent breakfast had been tucked away and the dishes washed.

Gus nodded. It was not in the nature of things that a youth's spirits should long remain at low ebb, and his tongue was beginning to loosen.

"Guess he's down by now, lying in camp and feeling as big as Alexander," the other went on. "And I don't blame him, either; only I wish it were we."

"You can be sure he's down," Gus spoke up at last. "It's mighty warm on that naked rock with the sun beating down on it at this time of year. That was our plan, you know, to go up early and come down early. And any man, sensible enough to get to the top, is bound to have sense enough to do it before the rock gets hot and his hands sweaty."

"And you can be sure he didn't take his shoes with, him." Hazard rolled over on his back and lazily regarded the speck of flag fluttering briskly on the sheer edge of the precipice. "Say!" He sat up with a start. "What's that?"

A metallic ray of light flashed out from the summit of Half Dome, then a second and a third. The heads of both boys were craned backward on the instant, agog with excitement.

"What a duffer!" Gus cried. "Why didn't he come down when it was cool?"

Hazard shook his head slowly, as if the question were too deep for immediate answer and they had better defer judgment.

The flashes continued, and as the boys soon noted, at irregular intervals of duration and disappearance. Now they were long, now short; and again they came and went with great rapidity, or ceased altogether for several moments at a time.

"I have it!" Hazard's face lighted up with the coming of understanding. "I have it! That fellow up there is trying to talk to us. He's flashing the sunlight down to us on a pocket-mirror—dot, dash; dot, dash; don't you see?"

The light also began to break in Gus's face. "Ah, I know! It's what they do in war-time—signaling. They call it heliographing, don't they? Same thing as telegraphing, only it's done without wires. And they use the same dots and dashes, too."

"Yes, the Morse alphabet. Wish I knew it."

"Same here. He surely must have something to say to us, or he wouldn't be kicking up all that rumpus."

Still the flashes came and went persistently, till Gus exclaimed: "That chap's in trouble, that's what's the matter with him! Most likely he's hurt himself or something or other."

"Go on!" Hazard scouted.

Gus got out the shotgun and fired both barrels three times in rapid succession. A perfect flutter of flashes came back before the echoes had ceased their antics. So unmistakable was the message that even doubting Hazard was convinced that the man who had forestalled them stood in some grave

16

danger.

"Quick, Gus," he cried, "and pack! I'll see to the horses. Our trip hasn't come to nothing, after all. We've got to go right up Half Dome and rescue him. Where's the map? How do we get to the Saddle?"

"'Taking the horse-trail below the Vernal Falls,'" Gus read from the guide-book, "'one mile of brisk traveling brings the tourist to the world-famed Nevada Fall. Close by, rising up in all its pomp and glory, the Cap of Liberty stands guard——"

"Skip all that!" Hazard impatiently interrupted. "The trail's what we want."

"Oh, here it is! 'Following the trail up the side of the fall will bring you to the forks. The left one leads to Little Yosemite Valley, Cloud's Rest, and other points.'"

"Hold on; that'll do! I've got it on the map now," again interrupted Hazard. "From the Cloud's Rest trail a dotted line leads off to Half Dome. That shows the trail's abandoned. We'll have to look sharp to find it. It's a day's journey."

"And to think of all that traveling, when right here we're at the bottom of the Dome!" Gus complained, staring up wistfully at the goal.

"That's because this is Yosemite, and all the more reason for us to hurry. Come on! Be lively, now!"

Well used as they were to trail life, but few minutes sufficed to see the camp equipage on the backs of the packhorses and the boys in the saddle. In the late twilight of that evening they hobbled their animals in a tiny mountain meadow, and cooked coffee and bacon for themselves at the very base of the Saddle. Here, also, before they turned into their blankets, they found the camp of the unlucky stranger who was destined to spend the night on the naked roof of the Dome.

Dawn was brightening into day when the panting lads threw themselves down at the summit of the Saddle and began taking off their shoes. Looking down from the great height, they seemed perched upon the ridgepole of the world, and even the snow-crowned Sierra peaks seemed beneath them. Directly below, on the one hand, lay Little Yosemite Valley, half a mile deep; on the other hand, Big Yosemite, a mile. Already the sun's rays were striking about the adventurers, but the darkness of night still shrouded the two great gulfs into which they peered. And above them, bathed in the full day, rose only the majestic curve of the Dome.

"What's that for?" Gus asked, pointing to a leather-shielded flask which Hazard was securely fastening in his shirt pocket.

"Dutch courage, of course," was the reply. "We'll need all our nerve in this undertaking, and a little bit more, and," he tapped the flask significantly, "here's the little bit more."

"Good idea," Gus commented.

How they had ever come possessed of this erroneous idea, it would be hard to discover; but they were young yet, and there remained for them many uncut pages of life. Believers, also, in the efficacy of whisky as a remedy for snake-bite, they had brought with them a fair supply of medicine-chest liquor. As yet they had not touched it.

"Have some before we start?" Hazard asked.

Gus looked into the gulf and shook his head. "Better wait till we get up higher and the climbing is more ticklish."

Some seventy feet above them projected the first eye-bolt. The winter accumulations of ice had twisted and bent it down till it did not stand more than a bare inch and a half above the rock—a most difficult object to lasso as such a distance. Time and again Hazard coiled his lariat in true cowboy fashion and made the cast, and time and again was he baffled by the elusive peg. Nor could Gus do better. Taking advantage of inequalities in the surface, they scrambled twenty feet up the Dome and found they could rest in a shallow crevice. The cleft side of the Dome was so near that they could look over its edge from the crevice and gaze down the smooth, vertical wall for nearly two thousand feet. It was yet too dark down below for them to see farther.

The peg was now fifty feet away, but the path they must cover to get to it was quite smooth, and ran at an inclination of nearly fifty degrees. It seemed impossible, in that intervening space, to find a resting-place. Either the climber must keep going up, or he must slide down; he could not stop. But just here rose the danger. The Dome was sphere-shaped, and if he should begin to slide, his course would be, not to the point from which he had started and where the Saddle would catch him, but off to the south toward Little Yosemite. This meant a plunge of half a mile.

"I'll try it," Gus said simply.

They knotted the two lariats together, so that they had over a hundred feet of rope between them; and then each boy tied an end to his waist.

"If I slide," Gus cautioned, "come in on the slack and brace yourself. If you don't, you'll follow me, that's all!"

"Ay, ay!" was the confident response. "Better take a nip before you start?"

Gus glanced at the proffered bottle. He knew himself and of what he was capable. "Wait till I make the peg and you join me. All ready?"

"Ay."

He struck out like a cat, on all fours, clawing energetically as he urged his upward progress, his comrade paying out the rope carefully. At first his speed was good, but gradually it dwindled. Now he was fifteen feet from the peg, now ten, now eight—but going, oh, so slowly! Hazard, looking up from his crevice, felt a contempt for him and disappointment in him. It did look easy. Now Gus was five feet away, and after a painful effort, four feet. But when only a yard intervened, he came to a standstill—not exactly a standstill, for, like a squirrel in a wheel, he maintained his position on the face of the Dome by the most desperate clawing.

He had failed, that was evident. The question now was, how to save himself. With a sudden, catlike movement he whirled over on his back, caught his heel in a tiny, saucer-shaped depression and sat up. Then his courage failed him. Day had at last penetrated to the floor of the valley, and he was appalled at the frightful distance.

"Go ahead and make it!" Hazard ordered; but Gus merely shook his head.

"Then come down!"

Again he shook his head. This was his ordeal, to sit, nerveless and insecure, on the brink of the precipice. But Hazard, lying safely in his crevice, now had to face his own ordeal, but one of a different nature. When Gus began to slide—as he soon must—would he, Hazard, be able to take in the slack and then meet the shock as the other tautened the rope and darted toward the plunge? It seemed doubtful. And there he lay, apparently safe, but in reality harnessed to death. Then rose the temptation. Why not cast off the rope about his waist? He would be safe at all events. It was a simple way out of the difficulty. There was no need that two should perish. But it was impossible for such temptation to overcome his pride of race, and his own pride in himself and in his honor. So the rope remained about him.

"Come down!" he ordered; but Gus seemed to have become petrified.

"Come down," he threatened, "or I'll drag you down!" He pulled on the rope to show he was in earnest.

"Don't you dare!" Gus articulated through his clenched teeth.

"Sure, I will, if you don't come!" Again he jerked the rope.

With a despairing gurgle Gus started, doing his best to work sideways from the plunge. Hazard, every sense on the alert, almost exulting in his perfect coolness, took in the slack with deft rapidity. Then, as the rope began to tighten, he braced himself. The shock drew him half out of the crevice; but he held firm and served as the center of the circle, while Gus, with the rope as a radius, described the circumference and ended up on the extreme southern edge of the Saddle. A few moments later Hazard was offering him the flask.

"Take some yourself," Gus said.

"No; you. I don't need it."

"And I'm past needing it." Evidently Gus was dubious of the bottle and its contents.

Hazard put it away in his pocket. "Are you game," he asked, "or are you going to give it up?"

"Never!" Gus protested. "I am game. No Lafee ever showed the white feather yet. And if I did lose my grit up there, it was only for the moment—sort of like seasickness. I'm all right now, and I'm going to the top."

"Good!" encouraged Hazard. "You lie in the crevice this time, and I'll show you how easy it is."

But Gus refused. He held that it was easier and safer for him to try again, arguing that it was less difficult for his one hundred and sixteen pounds to cling to the smooth rock than for Hazard's one hundred and sixty-five; also that it was easier for one hundred and sixty-five pounds to bring a sliding one hundred and sixteen to a stop than vice versa. And further, that he had the benefit of his previous experience. Hazard saw the justice of this, although it was with great reluctance that he gave in.

Success vindicated Gus's contention. The second time, just as it seemed as if his slide would be repeated, he made a last supreme effort and gripped the coveted peg. By means of the rope, Hazard quickly joined him. The next peg was nearly sixty feet away; but for nearly half that distance the base of some glacier in the forgotten past had ground a shallow furrow. Taking advantage of this, it was easy for Gus to lasso the eye-bolt. And it seemed, as was really the case, that the hardest part of the task was over. True, the curve steepened to nearly sixty degrees above them, but a comparatively unbroken line of eye-bolts, six feet apart, awaited the lads. They no longer had even to use the lasso. Standing on one peg it was child's play to throw the bight of the rope over the next and to draw themselves up to it.

A bronzed and bearded man met them at the top and gripped their hands in hearty fellowship.

"Talk about your Mont Blancs!" he exclaimed, pausing in the midst of greeting them to survey the mighty panorama. "But there's nothing

21

on all the earth, nor over it, nor under it, to compare with this!" Then he recollected himself and thanked them for coming to his aid. No, he was not hurt or injured in any way. Simply because of his own carelessness, just as he had arrived at the top the previous day, he had dropped his climbing rope. Of course it was impossible to descend without it. Did they understand heliographing? No? That was strange! How did they——

"Oh, we knew something was the matter," Gus interrupted, "from the way you flashed when we fired off the shotgun."

"Find it pretty cold last night without blankets?" Hazard queried.

"I should say so. I've hardly thawed out yet."

"Have some of this." Hazard shoved the flask over to him.

The stranger regarded him quite seriously for a moment, then said, "My dear fellow, do you see that row of pegs? Since it is my honest intention to climb down them very shortly, I am forced to decline. No, I don't think I'll have any, though I thank you just the same."

Hazard glanced at Gus and then put the flask back in his pocket. But when they pulled the doubled rope through the last eye-bolt and set foot on the Saddle, he again drew out the bottle.

"Now that we're down, we don't need it," he remarked, pithily. "And I've about come to the conclusion that there isn't very much in Dutch courage, after all." He gazed up the great curve of the Dome. "Look at what we've done without it!"

Several seconds thereafter a party of tourists, gathered at the margin of Mirror Lake, were astounded at the unwonted phenomenon of a whisky flask descending upon them like a comet out of a clear sky; and all the way back to the hotel they marveled greatly at the wonders of nature, especially meteorites.

TYPHOON OFF THE COAST OF JAPAN

Jack London's first story, published at the age of seventeen

It was four bells in the morning watch. We had just finished breakfast when the order came forward for the watch on deck to stand by to heave her to and all hands stand by the boats.

"Port! hard a port!" cried our sailing-master. "Clew up the topsails! Let the flying jib run down! Back the jib over to windward and run down the foresail!" And so was our schooner Sophie Sutherland hove to off the Japan coast, near Cape Jerimo, on April 10, 1893.

Then came moments of bustle and confusion. There were eighteen men to man the six boats. Some were hooking on the falls, others casting off the lashings; boat-steerers appeared with boat-compasses and water-breakers, and boat-pullers with the lunch boxes. Hunters were staggering under two or three shotguns, a rifle and heavy ammunition box, all of which were soon stowed away with their oilskins and mittens in the boats.

The sailing-master gave his last orders, and away we went, pulling three pairs of oars to gain our positions. We were in the weather boat, and so had a longer pull than the others. The first, second, and third lee boats soon had all sail set and were running off to the southward and westward with the wind beam, while the schooner was running off to leeward of them, so that in case of accident the boats would have fair wind home.

It was a glorious morning, but our boat-steerer shook his head ominously as he glanced at the rising sun and prophetically muttered: "Red sun in the morning, sailor take warning." The sun had an angry look, and a few light, fleecy "nigger-heads" in that quarter seemed abashed and frightened and soon disappeared.

Away off to the northward Cape Jerimo reared its black, forbidding head like some huge monster rising from the deep. The winter's snow, not yet entirely dissipated by the sun, covered it in patches of glistening white, over which the light wind swept on its way out to sea. Huge gulls rose slowly, fluttering their wings in the light breeze and striking their webbed feet on the surface of the water for over half a mile before they could leave it. Hardly had the patter, patter died away when a flock of sea quail rose, and with whistling wings flew away to windward, where members of a large band of whales were disporting themselves, their blowings sounding like the exhaust of steam engines. The harsh, discordant cries of a sea-parrot grated unpleasantly on the ear, and set half a dozen alert in a small band of seals that were ahead of us. Away they went, breaching and jumping entirely out of water. A sea-gull with slow, deliberate flight and long, majestic curves circled round us, and as a reminder of home a little English sparrow perched impudently on the fo'castle head, and, cocking his head on one side, chirped merrily. The boats were soon among the seals, and the bang! bang! of the guns could be heard from down to leeward.

The wind was slowly rising, and by three o'clock as, with a dozen seals in our boat, we were deliberating whether to go on or turn back, the recall flag was run up at the schooner's mizzen—a sure sign that with the rising wind the barometer was falling and that our sailing-master was getting anxious for the welfare of the boats.

Away we went before the wind with a single reef in our sail. With clenched teeth sat the boat-steerer, grasping the steering oar firmly with both hands, his restless eyes on the alert—a glance at the schooner ahead, as we rose on a sea, another at the mainsheet, and then one astern where the dark ripple of the wind on the water told him of a coming puff or a large white-cap that threatened to overwhelm us. The waves were holding high carnival, performing the strangest antics, as with wild glee they danced along in fierce pursuit—now up, now down, here, there, and everywhere, until some great sea of liquid green with its milk-white crest of foam rose from the ocean's throbbing bosom and drove the others from view. But only for a moment, for again under new forms they reappeared. In the sun's path they wandered, where every ripple, great or small, every little spit or spray looked like molten silver, where the water lost its dark green color and became a dazzling, silvery flood, only to vanish and become a wild waste of sullen turbulence, each dark foreboding sea rising and breaking, then rolling on again. The dash, the sparkle, the silvery light soon vanished with the sun, which became obscured by black clouds that were rolling swiftly in from the west, northwest; apt heralds of the coming storm.

We soon reached the schooner and found ourselves the last aboard. In a few minutes the seals were skinned, boats and decks washed, and we were down below by the roaring fo'castle fire, with a wash, change of clothes, and a hot, substantial supper before us. Sail had been put on the schooner, as we had a run of seventy-five miles to make to the southward before morning, so as to get in the midst of the seals, out of which we had strayed during the last two days' hunting.

We had the first watch from eight to midnight. The wind was soon blowing half a gale, and our sailing-master expected little sleep that night as he paced up and down the poop. The topsails were soon clewed up and made fast, then the flying jib run down and furled. Quite a sea was rolling by this time, occasionally breaking over the decks, flooding them and threatening to smash the boats. At six bells we were ordered to turn them over and put on storm lashings. This occupied us till eight bells, when we were relieved by the mid-watch. I was the last to go below, doing so just as the watch on deck was furling the spanker. Below all were asleep except our green hand, the "bricklayer," who was dying of consumption. The wildly dancing movements of the sea lamp cast a pale, flickering light through the fo'castle and turned to golden honey the drops of water on the yellow oilskins. In all the corners dark shadows seemed to come and go, while up in the eyes of her, beyond the pall bits, descending from deck to deck, where they seemed to lurk like some dragon at the cavern's mouth, it was dark as Erebus. Now and again, the light seemed to penetrate for a moment as the schooner rolled heavier than usual, only to recede, leaving it darker and blacker than before. The roar of the wind through the rigging came to the ear muffled like the distant rumble of a train crossing a trestle or the surf on the beach, while the loud crash of the seas on her weather bow seemed almost to rend the beams and planking asunder as it resounded through the fo'castle. The creaking and groaning of the timbers, stanchions, and bulkheads, as the strain the vessel was undergoing was felt, served to drown the groans of the dying man as he tossed uneasily in his bunk. The working of the foremast against the deck beams caused a shower of flaky powder to fall, and sent another sound mingling with the tumultous storm. Small cascades of water streamed from the pall bits from the fo'castle head above, and, joining issue with the streams from the wet oilskins, ran along the floor and disappeared aft into the main hold.

At two bells in the middle watch—that is, in land parlance one o'clock in the morning—the order was roared out on the fo'castle: "All hands on deck and shorten sail!"

Then the sleepy sailors tumbled out of their bunk and into their clothes, oil-skins, and sea-boots and up on deck. 'Tis when that order comes on cold, blustering nights that "Jack" grimly mutters: "Who would not sell a farm and go to sea?"

It was on deck that the force of the wind could be fully appreciated, especially after leaving the stifling fo'castle. It seemed to stand up against you like a wall, making it almost impossible to move on the heaving decks or to breathe as the fierce gusts came dashing by. The schooner was hove to under jib, foresail, and mainsail. We proceeded to lower the foresail and make it fast. The night was dark, greatly impeding our labor. Still, though not a star or the moon could pierce the black masses of storm clouds that obscured the sky as they swept along before the gale, nature aided us in a measure. A soft light emanated from the movement of the ocean. Each mighty sea, all phosphorescent and glowing with the tiny lights of myriads of animalculæ, threatened to overwhelm us with a deluge of fire. Higher and higher, thinner and thinner, the crest grew as it began to curve and overtop preparatory to breaking, until with a roar it fell over the bulwarks, a mass of soft glowing light and tons of water which sent the sailors sprawling in all directions and left in each nook and cranny little specks of light that glowed and trembled till the next sea washed them away, depositing new ones in their places. Sometimes several seas following each other with great rapidity and thundering down on our decks filled them full to the bulwarks, but soon they were discharged through the lee scuppers.

To reef the mainsail we were forced to run off before the gale under the single reefed jib. By the time we had finished the wind had forced up such a tremendous sea that it was impossible to heave her to. Away we flew on the wings of the storm through the muck and flying spray. A wind sheer to starboard, then another to port as the enormous seas struck the schooner astern and nearly broached her to. As day broke we took in the jib, leaving not a sail unfurled. Since we had begun scudding she had ceased to take the seas over her bow, but amidships they broke fast and furious. It was a dry storm in the matter of rain, but the force of the wind filled the air with fine spray, which flew as high as the crosstrees and cut the face like a knife, making it impossible to see over a hundred yards ahead. The sea was a dark lead color as with long, slow, majestic roll it was heaped up by the wind into liquid mountains of foam. The wild antics of the schooner were sickening as she forged along. She would almost stop, as though climbing a mountain, then rapidly rolling to right and left as she gained the summit of a huge sea, she steadied herself and paused for a moment as though affrighted at the yawning precipice before her. Like an avalanche, she shot forward and down as the sea astern struck her with the force of a thousand battering rams, burying her bow to the catheads in the milky foam at the bottom that came on deck in all directions—forward, astern, to right and left, through the hawse-pipes and over the rail.

The wind began to drop, and by ten o'clock we were talking of heaving her to. We passed a ship, two schooners, and a four-masted barkentine under the smallest of canvas, and at eleven o'clock, running up the spanker and jib, we hove her to, and in another hour we were beating back again against the aftersea under full sail to regain the sealing ground away to the westward.

Below, a couple of men were sewing the "bricklayer's" body in canvas preparatory to the sea burial. And so with the storm passed away the "bricklayer's" soul.

THE LOST POACHER

"But they won't take excuses. You're across the line, and that's enough. They'll take you. In you go, Siberia and the salt-mines. And as for Uncle Sam, why, what's he to know about it? Never a word will get back to the States. 'The Mary Thomas,' the papers will say, 'the Mary Thomas lost with all hands. Probably in a typhoon in the Japanese seas.' That's what the papers will say, and people, too. In you go, Siberia and the salt-mines. Dead to the world and kith and kin, though you live fifty years."

In such manner John Lewis, commonly known as the "sea-lawyer," settled the matter out of hand.

It was a serious moment in the forecastle of the Mary Thomas. No sooner had the watch below begun to talk the trouble over, than the watch on deck came down and joined them. As there was no wind, every hand could be spared with the exception of the man at the wheel, and he remained only for the sake of discipline. Even "Bub" Russell, the cabin-boy, had crept forward to hear what was going on.

However, it was a serious moment, as the grave faces of the sailors bore witness. For the three preceding months the Mary Thomas sealing schooner, had hunted the seal pack along the coast of Japan and north to Bering Sea. Here, on the Asiatic side of the sea, they were forced to give over the chase, or rather, to go no farther; for beyond, the Russian cruisers patrolled forbidden ground, where the seals might breed in peace.

A week before she had fallen into a heavy fog accompanied by calm. Since then the fog-bank had not lifted, and the only wind had been light airs and catspaws. This in itself was not so bad, for the sealing schooners are never in a hurry so long as they are in the midst of the seals; but the trouble lay in the fact that the current at this point bore heavily to the north. Thus the Mary Thomas had unwittingly drifted across the line, and every hour she was penetrating, unwillingly, farther and farther into the dangerous waters where the Russian bear kept guard.

How far she had drifted no man knew. The sun had not been visible for a week, nor the stars, and the captain had been unable to take observations in order to determine his position. At any moment a cruiser might swoop down and hale the crew away to Siberia. The fate of other poaching seal-hunters was too well known to the men of the Mary Thomas, and there was cause for grave faces.

"Mine friends," spoke up a German boat-steerer, "it vas a pad piziness. Shust as ve make a big catch, und all honest, somedings go wrong, und der Russians nab us, dake our skins and our schooner, und send us mit der anarchists to Siberia. Ach! a pretty pad piziness!"

"Yes, that's where it hurts," the sea lawyer went on. "Fifteen hundred skins in the salt piles, and all honest, a big pay-day coming to every man Jack of us, and then to be captured and lose it all! It'd be different if we'd been poaching, but it's all honest work in open water."

"But if we haven't done anything wrong, they can't do anything to us, can they?" Bub queried.

"It strikes me as 'ow it ain't the proper thing for a boy o' your age shovin' in when 'is elders is talkin'," protested an English sailor, from over the edge of his bunk.

"Oh, that's all right, Jack," answered the sea-lawyer. "He's a perfect right to. Ain't he just as liable to lose his wages as the rest of us?"

"Wouldn't give thruppence for them!" Jack sniffed back. He had been planning to go home and see his family in Chelsea when he was paid off, and he was now feeling rather blue over the highly possible loss, not only of his pay, but of his liberty.

"How are they to know?" the sea-lawyer asked in answer to Bub's previous question. "Here we are in forbidden water. How do they know but what we came here of our own accord? Here we are, fifteen hundred skins in the hold. How do they, know whether we got them in open water or in the closed sea? Don't you see, Bub, the evidence is all against us. If you caught a man with his pockets full of apples like those which grow on your tree, and if you caught him in your tree besides, what'd you think if he told you he couldn't help it, and had just been sort of blown there, and that anyway those apples came from some other tree—what'd you think, eh?"

Bub saw it clearly when put in that light, and shook his head despondently.

"You'd rather be dead than go to Siberia," one of the boat-pullers said. "They put you into the salt-mines and work you till you die. Never see daylight again. Why, I've heard tell of one fellow that was chained to his mate, and that mate died. And they were both chained together! And if they send you to the quicksilver mines you get salivated. I'd rather be hung than salivated."

"Wot's salivated?" Jack asked, suddenly sitting up in his bunk at the hint of fresh misfortunes.

"Why, the quicksilver gets into your blood; I think that's the way. And your gums all swell like you had the scurvy, only worse, and your teeth get loose in your jaws. And big ulcers form, and then you die horrible. The strongest man can't last long a-mining quicksilver."

"A pad piziness," the boat-steerer reiterated, dolorously, in the silence which followed. "A pad piziness. I vish I was in Yokohama. Eh? Vot vas dot?"

The vessel had suddenly heeled over. The decks were aslant. A tin pannikin rolled down the inclined plane, rattling and banging. From above came the slapping of canvas and the quivering rat-tat-tat of the after leech of the loosely stretched foresail. Then the mate's voice sang down the hatch, "All hands on deck and make sail!"

Never had such summons been answered with more enthusiasm. The calm had broken. The wind had come which was to carry them south into safety. With a wild cheer all sprang on deck. Working with mad haste, they flung out topsails, flying jibs and stay-sails. As they worked, the fog-bank lifted and the black vault of heaven, bespangled with the old familiar stars, rushed into view. When all was ship-shape, the Mary Thomas was lying gallantly over on her side to a beam wind and plunging ahead due south.

"Steamer's lights ahead on the port bow, sir!" cried the lookout from his station on the forecastle-head. There was excitement in the man's voice.

The captain sent Bub below for his night-glasses. Everybody crowded to the lee-rail to gaze at the suspicious stranger, which already began to loom up vague and indistinct. In those unfrequented waters the chance was one in a thousand that it could be anything else than a Russian patrol. The captain was still anxiously gazing through the glasses, when a flash of flame left the stranger's side, followed by the loud report of a cannon. The worst fears were confirmed. It was a patrol, evidently firing across the bows of the Mary Thomas in order to make her heave to.

"Hard down with your helm!" the captain commanded the steers-man, all the life gone out of his voice. Then to the crew, "Back over the jib and foresail! Run down the flying jib! Clew up the foretopsail! And aft here and swing on to the main-sheet!"

The Mary Thomas ran into the eye of the wind, lost headway, and fell to courtesying gravely to the long seas rolling up from the west.

The cruiser steamed a little nearer and lowered a boat. The sealers watched in heartbroken silence. They could see the white bulk of the boat as it was slacked away to the water, and its crew sliding aboard. They could hear the creaking of the davits and the commands of the officers. Then the boat sprang away under the impulse of the oars, and came toward them. The wind had been rising, and already the sea was too rough to permit the frail craft to lie alongside the tossing schooner; but watching their chance, and taking advantage of the boarding ropes thrown to them, an officer and a couple of men clambered aboard. The boat then sheered off into safety and lay to its oars, a young midshipman, sitting in the stern and holding the yoke-lines, in charge.

The officer, whose uniform disclosed his rank as that of second lieutenant in the Russian navy, went below with the captain of the Mary Thomas to look at the ship's papers. A few minutes later he emerged, and upon his sailors removing the hatch-covers, passed down into the hold with a lantern to inspect the salt piles. It was a goodly heap which confronted him—fifteen hundred fresh skins, the season's catch; and under the circumstances he could have had but one conclusion.

"I am very sorry," he said, in broken English to the sealing captain, when he again came on deck, "but it is my duty, in the name of the tsar, to seize your vessel as a poacher caught with fresh skins in the closed sea. The penalty, as you may know, is confiscation and imprisonment."

The captain of the Mary Thomas shrugged his shoulders in seeming indifference, and turned away. Although they may restrain all outward show, strong men, under unmerited misfortune, are sometimes very close to tears. Just then the vision of his little California home, and of the wife and two yellow-haired boys, was strong upon him, and there was a strange, choking sensation in his throat, which made him afraid that if he attempted to speak he would sob instead.

And also there was upon him the duty he owed his men. No weakness before them, for he must be a tower of strength to sustain them in misfortune. He had already explained to the second lieutenant, and knew the hopelessness of the situation. As the sea-lawyer had said, the evidence was all against him. So he turned aft, and fell to pacing up and down the poop of the vessel over which he was no longer commander.

The Russian officer now took temporary charge. He ordered more of his men aboard, and had all the canvas clewed up and furled snugly away. While this was being done, the boat plied back and forth between the two vessels, passing a heavy hawser, which was made fast to the great towing-bitts on the schooner's forecastle-head. During all this work the sealers stood about in sullen groups. It was madness to think of resisting, with the guns of a man-of-war not a biscuit-toss away; but they refused to lend a hand, preferring instead to maintain a gloomy silence.

Having accomplished his task, the lieutenant ordered all but four of his men back into the boat. Then the midshipman, a lad of sixteen, looking strangely mature and dignified in his uniform and sword, came aboard to take command of the captured sealer. Just as the lieutenant prepared to depart, his eyes chanced to alight upon Bub. Without a word of warning, he seized him by the arm and dropped him over the rail into the waiting boat; and then, with a parting wave of his hand, he followed him.

It was only natural that Bub should be frightened at this unexpected happening. All the terrible stories he had heard of the Russians served to make him fear them, and now returned to his mind with double force. To be captured by them was bad enough, but to be carried off by them, away from his comrades, was a fate of which he had not dreamed.

"Be a good boy, Bub," the captain called to him, as the boat drew away from the Mary Thomas's side, "and tell the truth!"

"Aye, aye, sir!" he answered, bravely enough, by all outward appearance. He felt a certain pride of race, and was ashamed to be a coward before these strange enemies, these wild Russian bears.

"Und be politeful!" the German boat-steerer added, his rough voice lifting across the water like a fog-horn.

Bub waved his hand in farewell, and his mates clustered along the rail as they answered with a cheering shout. He found room in the stern-sheets, where he fell to regarding the lieutenant. He didn't look so wild or bearish, after all—very much like other men, Bub concluded, and the sailors were much the same as all other man-of-war's men he had ever known. Nevertheless, as his feet struck the steel deck of the cruiser, he felt as if he had entered the portals of a prison.

For a few minutes he was left unheeded. The sailors hoisted the boat up, and swung it in on the davits. Then great clouds of black smoke poured out of the funnels, and they were under way—to Siberia, Bub could not help but think. He saw the Mary Thomas swing abruptly into line as she took the pressure from the hawser, and her side-lights, red and green, rose and fell as she was towed through the sea.

Bub's eyes dimmed at the melancholy sight, but—but just then the lieutenant came to take him down to the commander, and he straightened up and set his lips firmly, as if this were a very commonplace affair and he were used to being sent to Siberia every day in the week. The cabin in which the commander sat was like a palace compared to the humble fittings of the Mary Thomas, and the commander himself, in gold lace and dignity, was a most august personage, quite unlike the simple man who navigated his schooner on the trail of the seal pack.

Bub now quickly learned why he had been brought aboard, and in the prolonged questioning which followed, told nothing but the plain truth. The truth was harmless; only a lie could have injured his cause. He did not know much, except that they had been sealing far to the south in open water, and that when the calm and fog came down upon them, being close to the line, they had drifted across. Again and again he insisted that they had not lowered a boat or shot a seal in the week they had been drifting about in the forbidden sea; but the commander chose to consider all that he said to be a tissue of falsehoods, and adopted a bullying tone in an effort to frighten the boy. He threatened and cajoled by turns, but failed in the slightest to shake Bub's statements, and at last ordered him out of his presence.

By some oversight, Bub was not put in anybody's charge, and wandered up on deck unobserved. Sometimes the sailors, in passing, bent curious glances upon him, but otherwise he was left strictly alone. Nor could he have attracted much attention, for he was small, the night dark, and the watch on deck intent on its own business. Stumbling over the strange decks, he made his way aft where he could look upon the side-lights of the Mary Thomas, following steadily in the rear.

For a long while he watched, and then lay down in the darkness close to where the hawser passed over the stern to the captured schooner. Once an officer came up and examined the straining rope to see if it were chafing, but Bub cowered away in the shadow undiscovered. This, however, gave him an idea which concerned the lives and liberties of twenty-two men, and which was to avert crushing sorrow from more than one happy home many thousand miles away.

In the first place, he reasoned, the crew were all guiltless of any crime, and yet were being carried relentlessly away to imprisonment in Siberia—a living death, he had heard, and he believed it implicitly. In the second place, he was a prisoner, hard and fast, with no chance of escape. In the third, it was possible for the twenty-two men on the Mary Thomas to escape. The only thing which bound them was a four-inch hawser. They dared not cut it at their end, for a watch was sure to be maintained upon it by their Russian captors; but at this end, ah! at his end——

Bub did not stop to reason further. Wriggling close to the hawser, he opened his jack-knife and went to work, The blade was not very sharp, and he sawed away, rope-yarn by rope-yarn, the awful picture of the solitary Siberian exile he must endure growing clearer and more terrible at every stroke. Such a fate was bad enough to undergo with one's comrades, but to face it alone seemed frightful. And besides, the very act he was performing was sure to bring greater punishment upon him.

In the midst of such somber thoughts, he heard footsteps approaching. He wriggled away into the shadow. An officer stopped where he had been working, half-stooped to examine the hawser, then changed his mind and straightened up. For a few minutes he stood there, gazing at the lights of the captured schooner, and then went forward again.

Now was the time! Bub crept back and went on sawing. Now two parts were severed. Now three. But one remained. The tension upon this was so great that it readily yielded. Splash! The freed end went overboard. He lay quietly, his heart in his mouth, listening. No one on the cruiser but himself had heard.

He saw the red and green lights of the Mary Thomas grow dimmer and dimmer. Then a faint hallo came over the water from the Russian prize crew. Still nobody heard. The smoke continued to pour out of the cruiser's funnels, and her propellers throbbed as mightily as ever.

What was happening on the Mary Thomas? Bub could only surmise; but of one thing he was certain: his comrades would assert themselves and overpower the four sailors and the midshipman. A few minutes later he saw a small flash, and straining his ears heard the very faint report of a pistol. Then, oh joy! both the red and green lights suddenly disappeared. The Mary Thomas was retaken!

Just as an officer came aft, Bub crept forward, and hid away in one of the boats. Not an instant too soon. The alarm was given. Loud voices rose in command. The cruiser altered her course. An electric search-light began to throw its white rays across the sea, here, there, everywhere; but in its flashing path no tossing schooner was revealed.

Bub went to sleep soon after that, nor did he wake till the gray of dawn. The engines were pulsing monotonously, and the water, splashing noisily, told him the decks were being washed down. One sweeping glance, and he saw that they were alone on the expanse of ocean. The Mary Thomas had escaped. As he lifted his head, a roar of laughter went up from the sailors. Even the officer, who ordered him taken below and locked up, could not quite conceal the laughter in his eyes. Bub thought often in the days of confinement which followed, that they were not very angry with him for what he had done.

He was not far from right. There is a certain innate nobility deep down in the hearts of all men, which forces them to admire a brave act, even if it is performed by an enemy. The Russians were in nowise different from other men. True, a boy had outwitted them; but they could not blame him, and they were sore puzzled as to what to do with him. It would never do to take a little mite like him in to represent all that remained of the lost poacher.

So, two weeks later, a United States man-of-war, steaming out of the Russian port of Vladivostok, was signaled by a Russian cruiser. A boat passed between the two ships, and a small boy dropped over the rail upon the deck of the American vessel. A week later he was put ashore at Hakodate, and after some telegraphing, his fare was paid on the railroad to Yokohama.

From the depot he hurried through the quaint Japanese streets to the harbor, and hired a sampan boatman to put him aboard a certain vessel whose familiar rigging had quickly caught his eye. Her gaskets were off, her sails unfurled; she was just starting back to the United States. As he came closer, a crowd of sailors sprang upon the forecastle head, and the windlass-bars rose and fell as the anchor was torn from its muddy bottom.

"'Yankee ship come down the ribber!'" the sea-lawyer's voice rolled out as he led the anchor song.

"'Pull, my bully boys, pull!'" roared back the old familiar chorus, the men's bodies lifting and bending to the rhythm.

Bub Russell paid the boatman and stepped on deck. The anchor was forgotten. A mighty cheer went up from the men, and almost before he could catch his breath he was on the shoulders of the captain, surrounded by his mates, and endeavoring to answer twenty questions to the second.

The next day a schooner hove to off a Japanese fishing village, sent ashore four sailors and a little midshipman, and sailed away. These men did not talk English, but they had money and quickly made their way to Yokohama. From that day the Japanese village folk never heard anything more about them, and they are still a much-talked-of mystery. As the Russian government never said anything about the incident, the United States is still ignorant of the whereabouts of the lost poacher, nor has she ever heard, officially, of the way in which some of her citizens "shanghaied" five subjects of the tsar. Even nations have secrets sometimes.

THE BANKS OF THE SACRAMENTO

"And it's blow, ye winds, heigh-ho,

For Cal-i-for-ni-o;

For there's plenty of gold so I've been told,

On the banks of the Sacramento!"

It was only a little boy, singing in a shrill treble the sea chantey which seamen sing the wide world over when they man the capstan bars and break the anchors out for "Frisco" port. It was only a little boy who had never seen the sea, but two hundred feet beneath him rolled the Sacramento. "Young" Jerry he was called, after "Old" Jerry, his father, from whom he had learned the song, as well as received his shock of bright-red hair, his blue, dancing eyes, and his fair and inevitably freckled skin.

For Old Jerry had been a sailor, and had followed the sea till middle life, haunted always by the words of the ringing chantey. Then one day he had sung the song in earnest, in an Asiatic port, swinging and thrilling round the capstan-circle with twenty others. And at San Francisco he turned his back upon his ship and upon the sea, and went to behold with his own eyes the banks of the Sacramento.

He beheld the gold, too, for he found employment at the Yellow Dream mine, and proved of utmost usefulness in rigging the great ore-cables across the river and two hundred feet above its surface.

After that he took charge of the cables and kept them in repair, and ran them and loved them, and became himself an indispensable fixture of the Yellow Dream mine. Then he loved pretty Margaret Kelly; but she had left him and Young Jerry, the latter barely toddling, to take up her last long sleep in the little graveyard among the great sober pines.

Old Jerry never went back to the sea. He remained by his cables, and lavished upon them and Young Jerry all the love of his nature. When evil days came to the Yellow-Dream, he still remained in the employ of the company as watchman over the all but abandoned property.

But this morning he was not visible. Young Jerry only was to be seen, sitting on the cabin step and singing the ancient chantey. He had cooked and eaten his breakfast all by himself, and had just come out to take a look at the world. Twenty feet before him stood the steel drum round which the endless cable worked. By the drum, snug and fast, was the ore-car. Following with his eyes the dizzy flight of the cables to the farther bank, he could see the other drum and the other car.

The contrivance was worked by gravity, the loaded car crossing the river by virtue of its own weight, and at the same time dragging the empty car back. The loaded car being emptied, and the empty car being loaded with more ore, the performance could be repeated—a performance which had been repeated tens of thousands of times since the day Old Jerry became the keeper of the cables.

Young Jerry broke off his song at the sound of approaching footsteps, A tall, blue-shirted man, a rifle across the hollow of his arm, came out from the gloom of the pine-trees. It was Hall, watchman of the Yellow Dragon mine, the cables of which spanned the Sacramento a mile farther up.

"Hello, younker!" was his greeting. "What you doin' here by your lonesome?"

"Oh, bachin'," Jerry tried to answer unconcernedly, as if it were a very ordinary sort of thing. "Dad's away, you see."

"Where's he gone?" the man asked.

"San Francisco. Went last night. His brother's dead in the old country, and he's gone down to see the lawyers. Won't be back till tomorrow night."

So spoke Jerry, and with pride, because of the responsibility which had fallen to him of keeping an eye on the property of the Yellow Dream, and the glorious adventure of living alone on the cliff above the river and of cooking his own meals.

"Well, take care of yourself," Hall said, "and don't monkey with the cables. I'm goin' to see if I can't pick up a deer in the Cripple Cow Cañon."

"It's goin' to rain, I think," Jerry said, with mature deliberation.

"And it's little I mind a wettin'," Hall laughed, as he strode away among the trees.

Jerry's prediction concerning rain was more than fulfilled. By ten o'clock the pines were swaying and moaning, the cabin windows rattling, and the rain driving by in fierce squalls. At half past eleven he kindled a fire, and promptly at the stroke of twelve sat down to his dinner.

No out-of-doors for him that day, he decided, when he had washed the few dishes and put them neatly away; and he wondered how wet Hall was and whether he had succeeded in picking up a deer.

At one o'clock there came a knock at the door, and when he opened it a man and a woman staggered in on the breast of a great gust of wind. They were Mr. and Mrs. Spillane, ranchers, who lived in a lonely valley a dozen miles back from the river.

"Where's Hall?" was Spillane's opening speech, and he spoke sharply and quickly.

Jerry noted that he was nervous and abrupt in his movements, and that Mrs. Spillane seemed laboring under some strong anxiety. She was a thin, washed-out, worked-out woman, whose life of dreary and unending toil had stamped itself harshly upon her face. It was the same life that had bowed her husband's shoulders and gnarled his hands and turned his hair to a dry and dusty gray.

"He's gone hunting up Cripple Cow," Jerry answered. "Did you want to cross?"

The woman began to weep quietly, while Spillane dropped a troubled exclamation and strode to the window. Jerry joined him in gazing out to where the cables lost themselves in the thick downpour.

It was the custom of the backwoods people in that section of country to cross the Sacramento on the Yellow Dragon cable. For this service a small toll was charged, which tolls the Yellow Dragon Company applied to the payment of Hall's wages.

"We've got to get across, Jerry," Spillane said, at the same time jerking his thumb over his shoulder in the direction of his wife. "Her father's hurt at the Clover Leaf. Powder explosion. Not expected to live. We just got word."

Jerry felt himself fluttering inwardly. He knew that Spillane wanted to cross on the Yellow Dream cable, and in the absence of his father he felt that he dared not assume such a responsibility, for the cable had never been used for passengers; in fact, had not been used at all for a long time.

"Maybe Hall will be back soon," he said.

Spillane shook his head, and demanded, "Where's your father?"

"San Francisco," Jerry answered, briefly.

Spillane groaned, and fiercely drove his clenched fist into the palm of the other hand. His wife was crying more audibly, and Jerry could hear her murmuring, "And daddy's dyin', dyin'!"

The tears welled up in his own eyes, and he stood irresolute, not knowing what he should do. But the man decided for him.

"Look here, kid," he said, with determination, "the wife and me are goin' over on this here cable of yours! Will you run it for us?"

Jerry backed slightly away. He did it unconsciously, as if recoiling instinctively from something unwelcome.

"Better see if Hall's back," he suggested.

"And if he ain't?"

Again Jerry hesitated.

"I'll stand for the risk," Spillane added. "Don't you see, kid, we've simply got to cross!"

Jerry nodded his head reluctantly.

"And there ain't no use waitin' for Hall," Spillane went on. "You know as well as me he ain't back from Cripple Cow this time of day! So come along and let's get started."

No wonder that Mrs. Spillane seemed terrified as they helped her into the ore-car—so Jerry thought, as he gazed into the apparently fathomless gulf beneath her. For it was so filled with rain and cloud, hurtling and curling in the fierce blast, that the other shore, seven hundred feet away, was invisible, while the cliff at their feet dropped sheer down and lost itself in the swirling vapor. By all appearances it might be a mile to bottom instead of two hundred feet.

"All ready?" he asked.

"Let her go!" Spillane shouted, to make himself heard above the roar of the wind.

He had clambered in beside his wife, and was holding one of her hands in his.

Jerry looked upon this with disapproval. "You'll need all your hands for holdin' on, the way the wind's yowlin.'"

The man and the woman shifted their hands accordingly, tightly gripping the sides of the car, and Jerry slowly and carefully released the brake. The drum began to revolve as the endless cable passed round it, and the car slid slowly out into the chasm, its trolley wheels rolling on the stationary cable overhead, to which it was suspended.

It was not the first time Jerry had worked the cable, but it was the first time he had done so away from the supervising eye of his father. By means of the brake he regulated the speed of the car. It needed regulating, for at times, caught by the stronger gusts of wind, it swayed violently back and forth; and once, just before it was swallowed up in a rain squall, it seemed about to spill out its human contents.

After that Jerry had no way of knowing where the car was except by means of the cable. This he watched keenly as it glided around the drum.

"Three hundred feet," he breathed to himself, as the cable markings went by, "three hundred and fifty, four hundred; four hundred and——"

The cable had stopped. Jerry threw off the brake, but it did not move. He caught the cable with his hands and tried to start it by tugging smartly. Something had gone wrong. What? He could not guess; he could not see. Looking up, he could vaguely make out the empty car, which had been crossing from the opposite cliff at a speed equal to that of the loaded car. It was about two hundred and fifty feet away. That meant, he knew, that somewhere in the gray obscurity, two hundred feet above the river and two hundred and fifty feet from the other bank, Spillane and his wife were suspended and stationary.

Three times Jerry shouted with all the shrill force of his lungs, but no answering cry came out of the storm. It was impossible for him to hear them or to make himself heard. As he stood for a moment, thinking rapidly, the flying clouds seemed to thin and lift. He caught a brief glimpse of the swollen Sacramento beneath, and a briefer glimpse of the car and the man and woman. Then the clouds descended thicker than ever.

The boy examined the drum closely, and found nothing the matter with it. Evidently it was the drum on the other side that had gone wrong. He was appalled at thought of the man and woman out there in the midst of the storm, hanging over the abyss, rocking back and forth in the frail car and ignorant of what was taking place on shore. And he did not like to think of their hanging there while he went round by the Yellow Dragon cable to the other drum.

But he remembered a block and tackle in the tool-house, and ran and brought it. They were double blocks, and he murmured aloud, "A purchase of four," as he made the tackle fast to the endless cable. Then he heaved upon it, heaved until it seemed that his arms were being drawn out from their sockets and that his shoulder muscles would be ripped asunder. Yet the cable did not budge. Nothing remained but to cross over to the other side.

He was already soaking wet, so he did not mind the rain as he ran over the trail to the Yellow Dragon. The storm was with him, and it was easy going, although there was no Hall at the other end of it to man the brake for him

43

and regulate the speed of the car. This he did for himself, however, by means of a stout rope, which he passed, with a turn, round the stationary cable.

As the full force of the wind struck him in mid-air, swaying the cable and whistling and roaring past it, and rocking and careening the car, he appreciated more fully what must be the condition of mind of Spillane and his wife. And this appreciation gave strength to him, as, safely across, he fought his way up the other bank, in the teeth of the gale, to the Yellow Dream cable.

To his consternation, he found the drum in thorough working order. Everything was running smoothly at both ends. Where was the hitch? In the middle, without a doubt.

From this side, the car containing Spillane was only two hundred and fifty feet away. He could make out the man and woman through the whirling vapor, crouching in the bottom of the car and exposed to the pelting rain and the full fury of the wind. In a lull between the squalls he shouted to Spillane to examine the trolley of the car.

Spillane heard, for he saw him rise up cautiously on his knees, and with his hands go over both trolley-wheels. Then he turned his face toward the bank.

"She's all right, kid!"

Jerry heard the words, faint and far, as from a remote distance. Then what was the matter? Nothing remained but the other and empty car, which he could not see, but which he knew to be there, somewhere in that terrible gulf two hundred feet beyond Spillane's car.

His mind was made up on the instant. He was only fourteen years old, slightly and wirily built; but his life had been lived among the mountains, his father had taught him no small measure of "sailoring," and he was not particularly afraid of heights.

In the tool-box by the drum he found an old monkey-wrench and a short bar of iron, also a coil of fairly new Manila rope. He looked in vain for a piece of board with which to rig a "boatswain's chair." There was nothing at hand but large planks, which he had no means of sawing, so he was compelled to do without the more comfortable form of saddle.

The saddle he rigged was very simple. With the rope he made merely a large loop round the stationary cable, to which hung the empty car. When he sat in the loop his hands could just reach the cable conveniently, and where the rope was likely to fray against the cable he lashed his coat, in lieu of the old sack he would have used had he been able to find one.

These preparations swiftly completed, he swung out over the chasm, sitting in the rope saddle and pulling himself along the cable by his hands. With him he carried the monkey-wrench and short iron bar and a few spare feet of rope. It was a slightly up-hill pull, but this he did not mind so much as the wind. When the furious gusts hurled him back and forth, sometimes half twisting him about, and he gazed down into the gray depths, he was aware that he was afraid. It was an old cable. What if it should break under his weight and the pressure of the wind?

It was fear he was experiencing, honest fear, and he knew that there was a "gone" feeling in the pit of his stomach, and a trembling of the knees which he could not quell.

But he held himself bravely to the task. The cable was old and worn, sharp pieces of wire projected from it, and his hands were cut and bleeding by the time he took his first rest, and held a shouted conversation with Spillane. The car was directly beneath him and only a few feet away, so he was able to explain the condition of affairs and his errand.

"Wish I could help you," Spillane shouted at him as he started on, "but the wife's gone all to pieces! Anyway, kid, take care of yourself! I got myself in this fix, but it's up to you to get me out!"

"Oh, I'll do it!" Jerry shouted back. "Tell Mrs. Spillane that she'll be ashore now in a jiffy!"

In the midst of pelting rain, which half-blinded him, swinging from side to side like a rapid and erratic pendulum, his torn hands paining him severely and his lungs panting from his exertions and panting from the very air which the wind sometimes blew into his mouth with strangling force, he finally arrived at the empty car.

A single glance showed him that he had not made the dangerous journey in vain. The front trolley-wheel, loose from long wear, had jumped the cable, and the cable was now jammed tightly between the wheel and the sheave-block.

One thing was clear—the wheel must be removed from the block. A second thing was equally clear—while the wheel was being removed the car would have to be fastened to the cable by the rope he had brought.

At the end of a quarter of an hour, beyond making the car secure, he had accomplished nothing. The key which bound the wheel on its axle was rusted and jammed. He hammered at it with one hand and held on the best he could with the other, but the wind persisted in swinging and twisting his body, and made his blows miss more often than not. Nine-tenths of the strength he expended was in trying to hold himself steady. For fear that he might drop the monkey-wrench he made it fast to his wrist with his handkerchief.

At the end of half an hour Jerry had hammered the key clear, but he could not draw it out. A dozen times it seemed that he must give up in despair, that all the danger and toil he had gone through were for nothing. Then an idea came to him, and he went through his pockets with feverish haste, and found what he sought—a ten-penny nail.

But for that nail, put in his pocket he knew not when or why, he would have had to make another trip over the cable and back. Thrusting the nail through the looped head of the key, he at last had a grip, and in no time the key was out.

Then came punching and prying with the iron bar to get the wheel itself free from where it was jammed by the cable against the side of the block. After that Jerry replaced the wheel, and by means of the rope, heaved up on the car till the trolley once more rested properly on the cable.

All this took time. More than an hour and a half had elapsed since his arrival at the empty car. And now, for the first time, he dropped out of his saddle and down into the car. He removed the detaining ropes, and the trolley-wheels began slowly to revolve. The car was moving, and he knew that somewhere beyond, although he could not see, the car of Spillane was likewise moving, and in the opposite direction.

There was no need for a brake, for his weight sufficiently counterbalanced the weight in the other car; and soon he saw the cliff rising out of the cloud depths and the old familiar drum going round and round.

Jerry climbed out and made the car securely fast. He did it deliberately and carefully, and then, quite unhero-like, he sank down by the drum, regardless of the pelting storm, and burst out sobbing.

There were many reasons why he sobbed—partly from the pain of his hands, which was excruciating; partly from exhaustion; partly from relief and release from the nerve-tension he had been under for so long; and in a large measure from thankfulness that the man and woman were saved.

They were not there to thank him; but somewhere beyond that howling, storm-driven gulf he knew they were hurrying over the trail toward the Clover Leaf.

Jerry staggered to the cabin, and his hand left the white knob red with blood as he opened the door, but he took no notice of it.

He was too proudly contented with himself, for he was certain that he had done well, and he was honest enough to admit to himself that he had done well. But a small regret arose and persisted in his thoughts—if his father had only been there to see!

CHRIS FARRINGTON: ABLE SEAMAN

"If you vas in der old country ships, a liddle shaver like you vood pe only der boy, und you vood wait on der able seamen. Und ven der able seaman sing out, 'Boy, der water-jug!' you vood jump quick, like a shot, und bring der water-jug. Und ven der able seaman sing out, 'Boy, my boots!' you vood get der boots. Und you vood pe politeful, und say 'Yessir' und 'No sir.' But you pe in der American ship, und you t'ink you are so good as der able seamen. Chris, mine boy, I haf ben a sailorman for twenty-two years, und do you t'ink you are so good as me? I vas a sailorman pefore you vas borned, und I knot und reef und splice ven you play mit topstrings und fly kites."

"But you are unfair, Emil!" cried Chris Farrington, his sensitive face flushed and hurt. He was a slender though strongly built young fellow of seventeen, with Yankee ancestry writ large all over him.

"Dere you go vonce again!" the Swedish sailor exploded. "My name is Mister Johansen, und a kid of a boy like you call me 'Emil!' It vas insulting, und comes pecause of der American ship!"

"But you call me 'Chris!'" the boy expostulated, reproachfully.

"But you vas a boy."

"Who does a man's work," Chris retorted. "And because I do a man's work I have as much right to call you by your first name as you me. We are all equals in this fo'castle, and you know it. When we signed for the voyage in San Francisco, we signed as sailors on the Sophie Sutherland and there was no difference made with any of us. Haven't I always done my work? Did I ever shirk? Did you or any other man ever have to take a wheel for me? Or a lookout? Or go aloft?"

"Chris is right," interrupted a young English sailor. "No man has had to do a tap of his work yet. He signed as good as any of us, and he's shown himself as good—"

"Better!" broke in a Nova Scotia man. "Better than some of us! When we struck the sealing-grounds he turned out to be next to the best boat-steerer aboard. Only French Louis, who'd been at it for years, could beat him. I'm only a boat-puller, and you're only a boat-puller, too, Emil Johansen, for all your twenty-two years at sea. Why don't you become a boat-steerer?"

"Too clumsy," laughed the Englishman, "and too slow."

"Little that counts, one way or the other," joined in Dane Jurgensen, coming to the aid of his Scandinavian brother. "Emil is a man grown and an able seaman; the boy is neither."

And so the argument raged back and forth, the Swedes, Norwegians and Danes, because of race kinship, taking the part of Johansen, and the English, Canadians and Americans taking the part of Chris. From an unprejudiced point of view, the right was on the side of Chris. As he had truly said, he did a man's work, and the same work that any of them did. But they were prejudiced, and badly so, and out of the words which passed rose a standing quarrel which divided the forecastle into two parties.

The Sophie Sutherland was a seal-hunter, registered out of San Francisco, and engaged in hunting the furry sea-animals along the Japanese coast north to Bering Sea. The other vessels were two-masted schooners, but she was a three-master and the largest in the fleet. In fact, she was a full-rigged, three-topmast schooner, newly built.

Although Chris Farrington knew that justice was with him, and that he performed all his work faithfully and well, many a time, in secret thought, he longed for some pressing emergency to arise whereby he could demonstrate to the Scandinavian seamen that he also was an able seaman.

But one stormy night, by an accident for which he was in nowise accountable, in overhauling a spare anchor-chain he had all the fingers of his left hand badly crushed. And his hopes were likewise crushed, for it was impossible for him to continue hunting with the boats, and he was forced to stay idly aboard until his fingers should heal. Yet, although he little dreamed it, this very accident was to give him the long-looked-for opportunity.

49

One afternoon in the latter part of May the Sophie Sutherland rolled sluggishly in a breathless calm. The seals were abundant, the hunting good, and the boats were all away and out of sight. And with them was almost every man of the crew. Besides Chris, there remained only the captain, the sailing-master and the Chinese cook.

The captain was captain only by courtesy. He was an old man, past eighty, and blissfully ignorant of the sea and its ways; but he was the owner of the vessel, and hence the honorable title. Of course the sailing-master, who was really captain, was a thorough-going seaman. The mate, whose post was aboard, was out with the boats, having temporarily taken Chris's place as boat-steerer.

When good weather and good sport came together, the boats were accustomed to range far and wide, and often did not return to the schooner until long after dark. But for all that it was a perfect hunting day, Chris noted a growing anxiety on the part of the sailing-master. He paced the deck nervously, and was constantly sweeping the horizon with his marine glasses. Not a boat was in sight. As sunset arrived, he even sent Chris aloft to the mizzen-topmast-head, but with no better luck. The boats could not possibly be back before midnight.

Since noon the barometer had been falling with startling rapidity, and all the signs were ripe for a great storm—how great, not even the sailing-master anticipated. He and Chris set to work to prepare for it. They put storm gaskets on the furled topsails, lowered and stowed the foresail and spanker and took in the two inner jibs. In the one remaining jib they put a single reef, and a single reef in the mainsail.

Night had fallen before they finished, and with the darkness came the storm. A low moan swept over the sea, and the wind struck the Sophie Sutherland flat. But she righted quickly, and with the sailing-master at the wheel, sheered her bow into within five points of the wind. Working as well as he could with his bandaged hand, and with the feeble aid of the Chinese cook, Chris went forward and backed the jib over to the weather side. This with the flat mainsail, left the schooner hove to.

50

"God help the boats! It's no gale! It's a typhoon!" the sailing-master shouted to Chris at eleven o'clock. "Too much canvas! Got to get two more reefs into that mainsail, and got to do it right away!" He glanced at the old captain, shivering in oilskins at the binnacle and holding on for dear life. "There's only you and I, Chris—and the cook; but he's next to worthless!"

In order to make the reef, it was necessary to lower the mainsail, and the removal of this after pressure was bound to make the schooner fall off before the wind and sea because of the forward pressure of the jib.

"Take the wheel!" the sailing-master directed. "And when I give the word, hard up with it! And when she's square before it, steady her! And keep her there! We'll heave to again as soon as I get the reefs in!"

Gripping the kicking spokes, Chris watched him and the reluctant cook go forward into the howling darkness. The Sophie Sutherland was plunging into the huge head-seas and wallowing tremendously, the tense steel stays and taut rigging humming like harp-strings to the wind. A buffeted cry came to his ears, and he felt the schooner's bow paying off of its own accord. The mainsail was down!

He ran the wheel hard-over and kept anxious track of the changing direction of the wind on his face and of the heave of the vessel. This was the crucial moment. In performing the evolution she would have to pass broadside to the surge before she could get before it. The wind was blowing directly on his right cheek, when he felt the Sophie Sutherland lean over and begin to rise toward the sky—up—up—an infinite distance! Would she clear the crest of the gigantic wave?

Again by the feel of it, for he could see nothing, he knew that a wall of water was rearing and curving far above him along the whole weather side. There was an instant's calm as the liquid wall intervened and shut off the wind. The schooner righted, and for that instant seemed at perfect rest. Then she rolled to meet the descending rush.

Chris shouted to the captain to hold tight, and prepared himself for the shock. But the man did not live who could face it. An ocean of water smote

51

Chris's back and his clutch on the spokes was loosened as if it were a baby's. Stunned, powerless, like a straw on the face of a torrent, he was swept onward he knew not whither. Missing the corner of the cabin, he was dashed forward along the poop runway a hundred feet or more, striking violently against the foot of the foremast. A second wave, crushing inboard, hurled him back the way he had come, and left him half-drowned where the poop steps should have been.

Bruised and bleeding, dimly conscious, he felt for the rail and dragged himself to his feet. Unless something could be done, he knew the last moment had come. As he faced the poop, the wind drove into his mouth with suffocating force. This brought him back to his senses with a start. The wind was blowing from dead aft! The schooner was out of the trough and before it! But the send of the sea was bound to breach her to again. Crawling up the runway, he managed to get to the wheel just in time to prevent this. The binnacle light was still burning. They were safe!

That is, he and the schooner were safe. As to the welfare of his three companions he could not say. Nor did he dare leave the wheel in order to find out, for it took every second of his undivided attention to keep the vessel to her course. The least fraction of carelessness and the heave of the sea under the quarter was liable to thrust her into the trough. So, a boy of one hundred and forty pounds, he clung to his herculean task of guiding the two hundred straining tons of fabric amid the chaos of the great storm forces.

Half an hour later, groaning and sobbing, the captain crawled to Chris's feet. All was lost, he whimpered. He was smitten unto death. The galley had gone by the board, the mainsail and running-gear, the cook, everything!

"Where's the sailing-master?" Chris demanded when he had caught his breath after steadying a wild lurch of the schooner. It was no child's play to steer a vessel under single-reefed jib before a typhoon.

"Clean up for'ard," the old man replied. "Jammed under the fo'c'sle-head, but still breathing. Both his arms are broken, he says, and he doesn't know how many ribs. He's hurt bad."

"Well, he'll drown there the way she's shipping water through the hawse-pipes. Go for'ard!" Chris commanded, taking charge of things as a matter of course. "Tell him not to worry; that I'm at the wheel. Help him as much as you can, and make him help"—he stopped and ran the spokes to starboard as a tremendous billow rose under the stern and yawed the schooner to port—"and make him help himself for the rest. Unship the fo'castle hatch and get him down into a bunk. Then ship the hatch again."

The captain turned his aged face forward and wavered pitifully. The waist of the ship was full of water to the bulwarks. He had just come through it, and knew death lurked every inch of the way.

"Go!" Chris shouted, fiercely. And as the fear-stricken man started, "And take another look for the cook!"

Two hours later, almost dead from suffering, the captain returned. He had obeyed orders. The sailing-master was helpless, although safe in a bunk; the cook was gone. Chris sent the captain below to the cabin to change his clothes.

After interminable hours of toil, day broke cold and gray. Chris looked about him. The Sophie Sutherland was racing before the typhoon like a thing possessed. There was no rain, but the wind whipped the spray of the sea mast-high, obscuring everything except in the immediate neighborhood.

Two waves only could Chris see at a time—the one before and the one behind. So small and insignificant the schooner seemed on the long Pacific roll! Rushing up a maddening mountain, she would poise like a cockle-shell on the giddy summit, breathless and rolling, leap outward and down into the yawning chasm beneath, and bury herself in the smother of foam at the bottom. Then the recovery, another mountain, another sickening upward rush, another poise, and the downward crash. Abreast of him, to starboard, like a ghost of the storm, Chris saw the cook dashing apace with the schooner. Evidently, when washed overboard, he had grasped and become entangled in a trailing halyard.

For three hours more, alone with this gruesome companion, Chris held the Sophie Sutherland before the wind and sea. He had long since forgotten his mangled fingers. The bandages had been torn away, and the cold, salt spray had eaten into the half-healed wounds until they were numb and no longer pained. But he was not cold. The terrific labor of steering forced the perspiration from every pore. Yet he was faint and weak with hunger and exhaustion, and hailed with delight the advent on deck of the captain, who fed him all of a pound of cake-chocolate. It strengthened him at once.

He ordered the captain to cut the halyard by which the cook's body was towing, and also to go forward and cut loose the jib-halyard and sheet. When he had done so, the jib fluttered a couple of moments like a handkerchief, then tore out of the bolt-ropes and vanished. The Sophie Sutherland was running under bare poles.

By noon the storm had spent itself, and by six in the evening the waves had died down sufficiently to let Chris leave the helm. It was almost hopeless to dream of the small boats weathering the typhoon, but there is always the chance in saving human life, and Chris at once applied himself to going back over the course along which he had fled. He managed to get a reef in one of the inner jibs and two reefs in the spanker, and then, with the aid of the watch-tackle, to hoist them to the stiff breeze that yet blew. And all through the night, tacking back and forth on the back track, he shook out canvas as fast as the wind would permit.

The injured sailing-master had turned delirious and between tending him and lending a hand with the ship, Chris kept the captain busy. "Taught me more seamanship," as he afterward said, "than I'd learned on the whole voyage." But by daybreak the old man's feeble frame succumbed, and he fell off into exhausted sleep on the weather poop.

Chris, who could now lash the wheel, covered the tired man with blankets from below, and went fishing in the lazaretto for something to eat. But by the day following he found himself forced to give in, drowsing fitfully by the wheel and waking ever and anon to take a look at things.

On the afternoon of the third day he picked up a schooner, dismasted and battered. As he approached, close-hauled on the wind, he saw her decks crowded by an unusually large crew, and on sailing in closer, made out among others the faces of his missing comrades. And he was just in the nick of time, for they were fighting a losing fight at the pumps. An hour later they, with the crew of the sinking craft, were aboard the Sophie Sutherland.

Having wandered so far from their own vessel, they had taken refuge on the strange schooner just before the storm broke. She was a Canadian sealer on her first voyage, and as was now apparent, her last.

The captain of the Sophie Sutherland had a story to tell, also, and he told it well—so well, in fact, that when all hands were gathered together on deck during the dog-watch, Emil Johansen strode over to Chris and gripped him by the hand.

"Chris," he said, so loudly that all could hear, "Chris, I gif in. You vas yoost so good a sailorman as I. You vas a bully boy, und able seaman, und I pe proud for you!

"Und Chris!" He turned as if he had forgotten something, and called back, "From dis time always you call me 'Emil' mitout der 'Mister!'"

TO REPEL BOARDERS

"No; honest, now, Bob, I'm sure I was born too late. The twentieth century's no place for me. If I'd had my way——"

"You'd have been born in the sixteenth," I broke in, laughing, "with Drake and Hawkins and Raleigh and the rest of the sea-kings."

"You're right!" Paul affirmed. He rolled over upon his back on the little after-deck, with a long sigh of dissatisfaction.

It was a little past midnight, and, with the wind nearly astern, we were running down Lower San Francisco Bay to Bay Farm Island. Paul Fairfax and I went to the same school, lived next door to each other, and "chummed it" together. By saving money, by earning more, and by each of us foregoing a bicycle on his birthday, we had collected the purchase-price of the Mist, a beamy twenty-eight-footer, sloop-rigged, with baby topsail and centerboard. Paul's father was a yachtsman himself, and he had conducted the business for us, poking around, overhauling, sticking his penknife into the timbers, and testing the planks with the greatest care. In fact, it was on his schooner, the Whim, that Paul and I had picked up what we knew about boat-sailing, and now that the Mist was ours, we were hard at work adding to our knowledge.

The Mist, being broad of beam, was comfortable and roomy. A man could stand upright in the cabin, and what with the stove, cooking-utensils, and bunks, we were good for trips in her of a week at a time. And we were just starting out on the first of such trips, and it was because it was the first trip that we were sailing by night. Early in the evening we had beaten out from Oakland, and we were now off the mouth of Alameda Creek, a large salt-water estuary which fills and empties San Leandro Bay.

"Men lived in those days," Paul said, so suddenly as to startle me from my own thoughts. "In the days of the sea-kings, I mean," he explained.

I said "Oh!" sympathetically, and began to whistle "Captain Kidd."

"Now, I've my ideas about things," Paul went on. "They talk about romance and adventure and all that, but I say romance and adventure are dead. We're too civilized. We don't have adventures in the twentieth century. We go to the circus——"

"But——" I strove to interrupt, though he would not listen to me.

"You look here, Bob," he said. "In all the time you and I've gone together what adventures have we had? True, we were out in the hills once, and didn't get back till late at night, and we were good and hungry, but we weren't even lost. We knew where we were all the time. It was only a case of walk. What I mean is, we've never had to fight for our lives. Understand? We've never had a pistol fired at us, or a cannon, or a sword waving over our heads, or—or anything...."

"You'd better slack away three or four feet of that main-sheet," he said in a hopeless sort of way, as though it did not matter much anyway. "The wind's still veering around.

"Why, in the old times the sea was one constant glorious adventure," he continued. "A boy left school and became a midshipman, and in a few weeks was cruising after Spanish galleons or locking yard-arms with a French privateer, or—doing lots of things."

"Well—there are adventures today," I objected.

But Paul went on as though I had not spoken:

"And today we go from school to high school, and from high school to college, and then we go into the office or become doctors and things, and the only adventures we know about are the ones we read in books. Why, just as sure as I'm sitting here on the stern of the sloop Mist, just so sure am I that we wouldn't know what to do if a real adventure came along. Now, would we?"

"Oh, I don't know," I answered non-committally.

"Well, you wouldn't be a coward, would you?" he demanded.

I was sure I wouldn't and said so.

"But you don't have to be a coward to lose your head, do you?"

I agreed that brave men might get excited.

"Well, then," Paul summed up, with a note of regret in his voice, "the chances are that we'd spoil the adventure. So it's a shame, and that's all I can say about it."

"The adventure hasn't come yet," I answered, not caring to see him down in the mouth over nothing. You see, Paul was a peculiar fellow in some things, and I knew him pretty well. He read a good deal, and had a quick imagination, and once in a while he'd get into moods like this one. So I said, "The adventure hasn't come yet, so there's no use worrying about its being spoiled. For all we know, it might turn out splendidly."

Paul didn't say anything for some time, and I was thinking he was out of the mood, when he spoke up suddenly:

"Just imagine, Bob Kellogg, as we're sailing along now, just as we are, and never mind what for, that a boat should bear down upon us with armed men in it, what would you do to repel boarders? Think you could rise to it?"

"What would you do?" I asked pointedly. "Remember, we haven't even a single shotgun aboard."

"You would surrender, then?" he demanded angrily. "But suppose they were going to kill you?"

"I'm not saying what I'd do," I answered stiffly, beginning to get a little angry myself. "I'm asking what you'd do, without weapons of any sort?"

"I'd find something," he replied—rather shortly, I thought.

I began to chuckle. "Then the adventure wouldn't be spoiled, would it? And you've been talking rubbish."

Paul struck a match, looked at his watch, and remarked that it was nearly one o'clock—a way he had when the argument went against him. Besides, this was the nearest we ever came to quarreling now, though our share of squabbles had fallen to us in the earlier days of our friendship. I had just seen a little white light ahead when Paul spoke again.

"Anchor-light," he said. "Funny place for people to drop the hook. It may be a scow-schooner with a dinky astern, so you'd better go wide."

I eased the Mist several points, and, the wind puffing up, we went plowing along at a pretty fair speed, passing the light so wide that we could not make out what manner of craft it marked. Suddenly the Mist slacked up in a slow and easy way, as though running upon soft mud. We were both startled. The wind was blowing stronger than ever, and yet we were almost at a standstill.

"Mud-flat out here? Never heard of such a thing!"

So Paul exclaimed with a snort of unbelief, and, seizing an oar, shoved it down over the side. And straight down it went till the water wet his hand. There was no bottom! Then we were dumbfounded. The wind was whistling by, and still the Mist was moving ahead at a snail's pace. There seemed something dead about her, and it was all I could do at the tiller to keep her from swinging up into the wind.

"Listen!" I laid my hand on Paul's arm. We could hear the sound of rowlocks, and saw the little white light bobbing up and down and now very close to us. "There's your armed boat," I whispered in fun. "Beat the crew to quarters and stand by to repel boarders!"

We both laughed, and were still laughing when a wild scream of rage came out of the darkness, and the approaching boat shot under our stern. By the light of the lantern it carried we could see the two men in it distinctly. They were foreign-looking fellows with sun-bronzed faces, and with knitted tam-o'-shanters perched seaman fashion on their heads. Bright-colored woolen sashes were around their waists, and long sea-boots covered their legs. I remember yet the cold chill which passed along my backbone as I noted the tiny gold ear-rings in the ears of one. For all the world they were like pirates stepped out of the pages of romance. And, to make the picture complete, their faces were distorted with anger, and each flourished a long knife. They were both shouting, in high-pitched voices, some foreign jargon we could not understand.

One of them, the smaller of the two, and if anything the more vicious-looking, put his hands on the rail of the Mist and started to come aboard. Quick as a flash Paul placed the end of the oar against the man's chest and shoved him back into his boat. He fell in a heap, but scrambled to his feet, waving the knife and shrieking:

"You break-a my net-a! You break-a my net-a!"

And he held forth in the jargon again, his companion joining him, and both preparing to make another dash to come aboard the Mist.

"They're Italian fishermen," I cried, the facts of the case breaking in upon me. "We've run over their smelt-net, and it's slipped along the keel and fouled our rudder. We're anchored to it."

"Yes, and they're murderous chaps, too," Paul said, sparring at them with the oar to make them keep their distance.

"Say, you fellows!" he called to them. "Give us a chance and we'll get it clear for you! We didn't know your net was there. We didn't mean to do it, you know!"

"You won't lose anything!" I added. "We'll pay the damages!"

But they could not understand what we were saying, or did not care to understand.

"You break-a my net-a! You break-a my net-a!" the smaller man, the one with the earrings, screamed back, making furious gestures. "I fix-a you! You-a see, I fix-a you!"

This time, when Paul thrust him back, he seized the oar in his hands, and his companion jumped aboard. I put my back against the tiller, and no sooner had he landed, and before he had caught his balance, than I met him with another oar, and he fell heavily backward into the boat. It was getting serious, and when he arose and caught my oar, and I realized his strength, I confess that I felt a goodly tinge of fear. But though he was stronger than I,

60

instead of dragging me overboard when he wrenched on the oar, he merely pulled his boat in closer; and when I shoved, the boat was forced away. Besides, the knife, still in his right hand, made him awkward and somewhat counterbalanced the advantage his superior strength gave him. Paul and his enemy were in the same situation—a sort of deadlock, which continued for several seconds, but which could not last. Several times I shouted that we would pay for whatever damage their net had suffered, but my words seemed to be without effect.

Then my man began to tuck the oar under his arm, and to come up along it, slowly, hand over hand. The small man did the same with Paul. Moment by moment they came closer, and closer, and we knew that the end was only a question of time.

"Hard up, Bob!" Paul called softly to me.

I gave him a quick glance, and caught an instant's glimpse of what I took to be a very pale face and a very set jaw.

"Oh, Bob," he pleaded, "hard up your helm! Hard up your helm, Bob!"

And his meaning dawned upon me. Still holding to my end of the oar, I shoved the tiller over with my back, and even bent my body to keep it over. As it was the Mist was nearly dead before the wind, and this maneuver was bound to force her to jibe her mainsail from one side to the other. I could tell by the "feel" when the wind spilled out of the canvas and the boom tilted up. Paul's man had now gained a footing on the little deck, and my man was just scrambling up.

"Look out!" I shouted to Paul. "Here she comes!"

Both he and I let go the oars and tumbled into the cockpit. The next instant the big boom and the heavy blocks swept over our heads, the main-sheet whipping past like a great coiling snake and the Mist heeling over with a violent jar. Both men had jumped for it, but in some way the little man either got his knife-hand jammed or fell upon it, for the first sight we caught of him, he was standing in his boat, his bleeding fingers clasped close between his knees and his face all twisted with pain and helpless rage.

61

"Now's our chance!" Paul whispered. "Over with you!"

And on either side of the rudder we lowered ourselves into the water, pressing the net down with our feet, till, with a jerk, it went clear, Then it was up and in, Paul at the main-sheet and I at the tiller, the Mist plunging ahead with freedom in her motion, and the little white light astern growing small and smaller.

"Now that you've had your adventure, do you feel any better?" I remember asking when we had changed our clothes and were sitting dry and comfortable again in the cockpit.

"Well, if I don't have the nightmare for a week to come"—Paul paused and puckered his brows in judicial fashion—"it will be because I can't sleep, that's one thing sure!"

AN ADVENTURE IN THE UPPER SEA

I am a retired captain of the upper sea. That is to say, when I was a younger man (which is not so long ago) I was an aeronaut and navigated that aerial ocean which is all around about us and above us. Naturally it is a hazardous profession, and naturally I have had many thrilling experiences, the most thrilling, or at least the most nerve-racking, being the one I am about to relate.

It happened before I went in for hydrogen gas balloons, all of varnished silk, doubled and lined, and all that, and fit for voyages of days instead of mere hours. The "Little Nassau" (named after the "Great Nassau" of many years back) was the balloon I was making ascents in at the time. It was a fair-sized, hot-air affair, of single thickness, good for an hour's flight or so and capable of attaining an altitude of a mile or more. It answered my purpose, for my act at the time was making half-mile parachute jumps at recreation parks and country fairs. I was in Oakland, a California town, filling a summer's engagement with a street railway company. The company owned a large park outside the city, and of course it was to its interest to provide attractions which would send the townspeople over its line when they went out to get a whiff of country air. My contract called for two ascensions weekly, and my act was an especially taking feature, for it was on my days that the largest crowds were drawn.

Before you can understand what happened, I must first explain a bit about the nature of the hot air balloon which is used for parachute jumping. If you have ever witnessed such a jump, you will remember that directly the parachute was cut loose the balloon turned upside down, emptied itself of its smoke and heated air, flattened out and fell straight down, beating the parachute to the ground. Thus there is no chasing a big deserted bag for miles and miles across the country, and much time, as well as trouble, is thereby saved. This maneuver is accomplished by attaching a weight, at the end of a long rope, to the top of the balloon. The aeronaut, with his parachute and trapeze, hangs to the bottom of the balloon, and, weighing more, keeps it right side down. But when he lets go, the weight attached to the top immediately drags the top down, and the bottom, which is the open mouth, goes up, the heated air pouring out. The weight used for this purpose on the "Little Nassau" was a bag of sand.

On the particular day I have in mind there was an unusually large crowd in attendance, and the police had their hands full keeping the people back. There was much pushing and shoving, and the ropes were bulging with the pressure of men, women and children. As I came down from the dressing room I noticed two girls outside the ropes, of about fourteen and sixteen, and inside the rope a youngster of eight or nine. They were holding him by the hands, and he was struggling, excitedly and half in laughter, to get away from them. I thought nothing of it at the time—just a bit of childish play, no more; and it was only in the light of after events that the scene was impressed vividly upon me.

"Keep them cleared out, George!" I called to my assistant. "We don't want any accidents."

"Ay," he answered, "that I will, Charley."

George Guppy had helped me in no end of ascents, and because of his coolness, judgment and absolute reliability I had come to trust my life in his hands with the utmost confidence. His business it was to overlook the inflating of the balloon, and to see that everything about the parachute was in perfect working order.

The "Little Nassau" was already filled and straining at the guys. The parachute lay flat along the ground and beyond it the trapeze. I tossed aside my overcoat, took my position, and gave the signal to let go. As you know, the first rush upward from the earth is very sudden, and this time the balloon, when it first caught the wind, heeled violently over and was longer than usual in righting. I looked down at the old familiar sight of the world rushing away from me. And there were the thousands of people, every face silently upturned. And the silence startled me, for, as crowds went, this was the time for them to catch their first breath and send up a roar of applause. But there

64

was no hand-clapping, whistling, cheering—only silence. And instead, clear as a bell and distinct, without the slightest shake or quaver, came George's voice through the megaphone:

"Ride her down, Charley! Ride the balloon down!"

What had happened? I waved my hand to show that I had heard, and began to think. Had something gone wrong with the parachute? Why should I ride the balloon down instead of making the jump which thousands were waiting to see? What was the matter? And as I puzzled, I received another start. The earth was a thousand feet beneath, and yet I heard a child crying softly, and seemingly very close to hand. And though the "Little Nassau" was shooting skyward like a rocket, the crying did not grow fainter and fainter and die away. I confess I was almost on the edge of a funk, when, unconsciously following up the noise with my eyes, I looked above me and saw a boy astride the sandbag which was to bring the "Little Nassau" to earth. And it was the same little boy I had seen struggling with the two girls—his sisters, as I afterward learned.

There he was, astride the sandbag and holding on to the rope for dear life. A puff of wind heeled the balloon slightly, and he swung out into space for ten or a dozen feet, and back again, fetching up against the tight canvas with a thud which even shook me, thirty feet or more beneath. I thought to see him dashed loose, but he clung on and whimpered. They told me afterward, how, at the moment they were casting off the balloon, the little fellow had torn away from his sisters, ducked under the rope, and deliberately jumped astride the sandbag. It has always been a wonder to me that he was not jerked off in the first rush.

Well, I felt sick all over as I looked at him there, and I understood why the balloon had taken longer to right itself, and why George had called after me to ride her down. Should I cut loose with the parachute, the bag would at once turn upside down, empty itself, and begin its swift descent. The only hope lay in my riding her down and in the boy holding on. There was no possible way for me to reach him. No man could climb the slim, closed parachute; and even if a man could, and made the mouth of the balloon, what could he do? Straight out, and fifteen feet away, trailed the boy on his ticklish perch, and those fifteen feet were empty space.

I thought far more quickly than it takes to tell all this, and realized on the instant that the boy's attention must be called away from his terrible danger. Exercising all the self-control I possessed, and striving to make myself very calm, I said cheerily:

"Hello, up there, who are you!"

He looked down at me, choking back his tears and brightening up, but just then the balloon ran into a cross-current, turned half around and lay over. This set him swinging back and forth, and he fetched the canvas another bump. Then he began to cry again.

"Isn't it great?" I asked heartily, as though it was the most enjoyable thing in the world; and, without waiting for him to answer: "What's your name?"

"Tommy Dermott," he answered.

"Glad to make your acquaintance, Tommy Dermott," I went on. "But I'd like to know who said you could ride up with me?"

He laughed and said he just thought he'd ride up for the fun of it. And so we went on, I sick with fear for him, and cudgeling my brains to keep up the conversation. I knew that it was all I could do, and that his life depended upon my ability to keep his mind off his danger. I pointed out to him the great panorama spreading away to the horizon and four thousand feet beneath us. There lay San Francisco Bay like a great placid lake, the haze of smoke over the city, the Golden Gate, the ocean fog-rim beyond, and Mount Tamalpais over all, clear-cut and sharp against the sky. Directly below us I could see a buggy, apparently crawling, but I knew from experience that the men in it were lashing the horses on our trail.

But he grew tired of looking around, and I could see he was beginning to get frightened.

"How would you like to go in for the business?" I asked.

He cheered up at once and asked "Do you get good pay?"

But the "Little Nassau," beginning to cool, had started on its long descent, and ran into counter currents which bobbed it roughly about. This swung the boy around pretty lively, smashing him into the bag once quite severely. His lip began to tremble at this, and he was crying again. I tried to joke and laugh, but it was no use. His pluck was oozing out, and at any moment I was prepared to see him go shooting past me.

I was in despair. Then, suddenly, I remembered how one fright could destroy another fright, and I frowned up at him and shouted sternly:

"You just hold on to that rope! If you don't I'll thrash you within an inch of your life when I get you down on the ground! Understand?"

"Ye-ye-yes, sir," he whimpered, and I saw that the thing had worked. I was nearer to him than the earth, and he was more afraid of me than of falling.

"'Why, you've got a snap up there on that soft bag," I rattled on.

"Yes," I assured him, "this bar down here is hard and narrow, and it hurts to sit on it."

Then a thought struck him, and he forgot all about his aching fingers.

"When are you going to jump?" he asked. "That's what I came up to see."

I was sorry to disappoint him, but I wasn't going to make any jump.

But he objected to that. "It said so in the papers," he said.

"I don't care," I answered. "I'm feeling sort of lazy today, and I'm just going to ride down the balloon. It's my balloon and I guess I can do as I please about it. And, anyway, we're almost down now."

And we were, too, and sinking fast. And right there and then that youngster began to argue with me as to whether it was right for me to disappoint the people, and to urge their claims upon me. And it was with a happy heart that I held up my end of it, justifying myself in a thousand different ways, till we shot over a grove of eucalyptus trees and dipped to meet the earth.

"Hold on tight!" I shouted, swinging down from the trapeze by my hands in order to make a landing on my feet.

We skimmed past a barn, missed a mesh of clothesline, frightened the barnyard chickens into a panic, and rose up again clear over a haystack—all this almost quicker than it takes to tell. Then we came down in an orchard, and when my feet had touched the ground I fetched up the balloon by a couple of turns of the trapeze around an apple tree.

I have had my balloon catch fire in mid air, I have hung on the cornice of a ten-story house, I have dropped like a bullet for six hundred feet when a parachute was slow in opening; but never have I felt so weak and faint and sick as when I staggered toward the unscratched boy and gripped him by the arm.

"Tommy Dermott," I said, when I had got my nerves back somewhat. "Tommy Dermott, I'm going to lay you across my knee and give you the greatest thrashing a boy ever got in the world's history."

"No, you don't," he answered, squirming around. "You said you wouldn't if I held on tight."

"That's all right," I said, "but I'm going to, just the same. The fellows who go up in balloons are bad, unprincipled men, and I'm going to give you a lesson right now to make you stay away from them, and from balloons, too."

And then I gave it to him, and if it wasn't the greatest thrashing in the world, it was the greatest he ever got.

But it took all the grit out of me, left me nerve-broken, that experience. I canceled the engagement with the street railway company, and later on went in for gas. Gas is much the safer, anyway.

BALD-FACE

"Talkin' of bear——"

The Klondike King paused meditatively, and the group on the hotel porch hitched their chairs up closer.

"Talkin' of bear," he went on, "now up in the Northern Country there are various kinds. On the Little Pelly, for instance, they come down that thick in the summer to feed on the salmon that you can't get an Indian or white man to go nigher than a day's journey to the place. And up in the Rampart Mountains there's a curious kind of bear called the 'side-hill grizzly.' That's because he's traveled on the side-hills ever since the Flood, and the two legs on the down-hill side are twice as long as the two on the up-hill. And he can out-run a jack rabbit when he gets steam up. Dangerous? Catch you! Bless you, no. All a man has to do is to circle down the hill and run the other way. You see, that throws mister bear's long legs up the hill and the short ones down. Yes, he's a mighty peculiar creature, but that wasn't what I started in to tell about.

"They've got another kind of bear up on the Yukon, and his legs are all right, too. He's called the bald-face grizzly, and he's jest as big as he is bad. It's only the fool white men that think of hunting him. Indians got too much sense. But there's one thing about the bald-face that a man has to learn: he never gives the trail to mortal creature. If you see him comin', and you value your skin, you get out of his path. If you don't, there's bound to be trouble. If the bald-face met Jehovah Himself on the trail, he'd not give him an inch. O, he's a selfish beggar, take my word for it. But I had to learn all this. Didn't know anything about bear when I went into the country, exceptin' when I was a youngster I'd seen a heap of cinnamons and that little black kind. And they was nothin' to be scared at.

"Well, after we'd got settled down on our claim, I went up on the hill lookin' for a likely piece of birch to make an ax-handle out of. But it was pretty hard to find the right kind, and I kept a-goin' and kept a-goin' for nigh on two hours. Wasn't in no hurry to make my choice, you see, for I was headin' down to the Forks, where I was goin' to borrow a log-bit from Old Joe Gee. When I started, I'd put a couple of sour-dough biscuits and some sowbelly in my pocket in case I might get hungry. And I'm tellin' you that lunch came in right handy before I was done with it.

"Bime-by I hit upon the likeliest little birch saplin', right in the middle of a clump of jack pine. Jest as I raised my hand-ax I happened to cast my eyes down the hill. There was a big bear comin' up, swingin' along on all fours, right in my direction. It was a bald-face, but little I knew then about such kind.

"'Jest watch me scare him,' I says to myself, and I stayed out of sight in the trees.

"Well, I waited till he was about a hundred feet off, then out I runs into the open.

"'Oof! oof!' I hollered at him, expectin' to see him turn tail like chain lightning.

"Turn tail? He jest threw up his head for one good look and came a comin'.

"'Oof! oof!' I hollered, louder'n ever. But he jest came a comin'.

"'Consarn you!' I says to myself, gettin' mad. 'I'll make you jump the trail.'

"So I grabs my hat, and wavin' and hollerin' starts down the trail to meet him. A big sugar pine had gone down in a windfall and lay about breast high. I stops jest behind it, old bald-face comin' all the time. It was jest then that fear came to me. I yelled like a Comanche Indian as he raised up to come over the log, and fired my hat full in his face. Then I lit out.

"Say! I rounded the end of that log and put down the hill at a two-twenty clip, old bald-face reachin' for me at every jump. At the bottom was a broad, open flat, quarter of a mile to timber and full of niggerheads. I knew

70

if ever I slipped I was a goner, but I hit only the high places till you couldn't a-seen my trail for smoke. And the old devil snortin' along hot after me. Midway across, he reached for me, jest strikin' the heel of my moccasin with his claw. Tell you I was doin' some tall thinkin' jest then. I knew he had the wind of me and I could never make the brush, so I pulled my little lunch out of my pocket and dropped it on the fly.

"Never looked back till I hit the timber, and then he was mouthing the biscuits in a way which wasn't nice to see, considerin' how close he'd been to me. I never slacked up. No, sir! Jest kept hittin' the trail for all there was in me. But jest as I came around a bend, heelin' it right lively I tell you, what'd I see in middle of the trail before me, and comin' my way, but another bald-face!

"'Whoof!' he says when he spotted me, and he came a-runnin.'

"Instanter I was about and hittin' the back trail twice as fast as I'd come. The way this one was puffin' after me, I'd clean forgot all about the other bald-face. First thing I knew I seen him mosying along kind of easy, wonderin' most likely what had become of me, and if I tasted as good as my lunch. Say! when he seen me he looked real pleased. And then he came a-jumpin' for me.

"'Whoof!' he says.

"'Whoof!' says the one behind me.

"Bang I goes, slap off the trail sideways, a-plungin' and a-clawin' through the brush like a wild man. By this time I was clean crazed; thought the whole country was full of bald-faces. Next thing I knows—whop, I comes up against something in a tangle of wild blackberry bushes. Then that something hits me a slap and closes in on me. Another bald-face! And then and there I knew I was gone for sure. But I made up to die game, and of all the rampin' and roarin' and rippin' and tearin' you ever see, that was the worst.

"'My God! O my wife!' it says. And I looked and it was a man I was hammering into kingdom come.

"'Thought you was a bear,' says I.

"He kind of caught his breath and looked at me. Then he says, 'Same here.'

"Seemed as though he'd been chased by a bald-face, too, and had hid in the blackberries. So that's how we mistook each other.

"But by that time the racket on the trail was something terrible, and we didn't wait to explain matters. That afternoon we got Joe Gee and some rifles and came back loaded for bear. Mebbe you won't believe me, but when we got to the spot, there was the two bald-faces lyin' dead. You see, when I jumped out, they came together, and each refused to give trail to the other. So they fought it out. Talkin' of bear. As I was sayin'——"

IN YEDDO BAY

Somewhere along Theater Street he had lost it. He remembered being hustled somewhat roughly on the bridge over one of the canals that cross that busy thoroughfare. Possibly some slant-eyed, light-fingered pickpocket was even then enjoying the fifty-odd yen his purse had contained. And then again, he thought, he might have lost it himself, just lost it carelessly.

Hopelessly, and for the twentieth time, he searched in all his pockets for the missing purse. It was not there. His hand lingered in his empty hip-pocket, and he woefully regarded the voluble and vociferous restaurant-keeper, who insanely clamored: "Twenty-five sen! You pay now! Twenty-five sen!"

"But my purse!" the boy said. "I tell you I've lost it somewhere."

Whereupon the restaurant-keeper lifted his arms indignantly and shrieked: "Twenty-five sen! Twenty-five sen! You pay now!"

Quite a crowd had collected, and it was growing embarrassing for Alf Davis.

It was so ridiculous and petty, Alf thought. Such a disturbance about nothing! And, decidedly, he must be doing something. Thoughts of diving wildly through that forest of legs, and of striking out at whomsoever opposed him, flashed through his mind; but, as though divining his purpose, one of the waiters, a short and chunky chap with an evil-looking cast in one eye, seized him by the arm.

"You pay now! You pay now! Twenty-five sen!" yelled the proprietor, hoarse with rage.

Alf was red in the face, too, from mortification; but he resolutely set out on another exploration. He had given up the purse, pinning his last hope on stray coins. In the little change-pocket of his coat he found a ten-sen piece and five-copper sen; and remembering having recently missed a ten-sen piece, he cut the seam of the pocket and resurrected the coin from the depths of the lining. Twenty-five sen he held in his hand, the sum required to pay for the supper he had eaten. He turned them over to the proprietor, who counted them, grew suddenly calm, and bowed obsequiously—in fact, the whole crowd bowed obsequiously and melted away.

Alf Davis was a young sailor, just turned sixteen, on board the Annie Mine, an American sailing-schooner, which had run into Yokohama to ship its season's catch of skins to London. And in this, his second trip ashore, he was beginning to snatch his first puzzling glimpses of the Oriental mind. He laughed when the bowing and kotowing was over, and turned on his heel to confront another problem. How was he to get aboard ship? It was eleven o'clock at night, and there would be no ship's boats ashore, while the outlook for hiring a native boatman, with nothing but empty pockets to draw upon, was not particularly inviting.

Keeping a sharp lookout for shipmates, he went down to the pier. At Yokohama there are no long lines of wharves. The shipping lies out at anchor, enabling a few hundred of the short-legged people to make a livelihood by carrying passengers to and from the shore.

A dozen sampan men and boys hailed Alf and offered their services. He selected the most favorable-looking one, an old and beneficent-appearing man with a withered leg. Alf stepped into his sampan and sat down. It was quite dark and he could not see what the old fellow was doing, though he evidently was doing nothing about shoving off and getting under way. At last he limped over and peered into Alf's face.

"Ten sen," he said.

"Yes, I know, ten sen," Alf answered carelessly. "But hurry up. American schooner."

"Ten sen. You pay now," the old fellow insisted.

Alf felt himself grow hot all over at the hateful words "pay now." "You take me to American schooner; then I pay," he said.

But the man stood up patiently before him, held out his hand, and said,

"Ten sen. You pay now."

Alf tried to explain. He had no money. He had lost his purse. But he would pay. As soon as he got aboard the American schooner, then he would pay. No; he would not even go aboard the American schooner. He would call to his shipmates, and they would give the sampan man the ten sen first. After that he would go aboard. So it was all right, of course.

To all of which the beneficent-appearing old man replied: "You pay now. Ten sen." And, to make matters worse, the other sampan men squatted on the pier steps, listening.

Alf, chagrined and angry, stood up to step ashore. But the old fellow laid a detaining hand on his sleeve. "You give shirt now. I take you 'Merican schooner," he proposed.

Then it was that all of Alf's American independence flamed up in his breast. The Anglo-Saxon has a born dislike of being imposed upon, and to Alf this was sheer robbery! Ten sen was equivalent to six American cents, while his shirt, which was of good quality and was new, had cost him two dollars.

He turned his back on the man without a word, and went out to the end of the pier, the crowd, laughing with great gusto, following at his heels. The majority of them were heavy-set, muscular fellows, and the July night being one of sweltering heat, they were clad in the least possible raiment. The water-people of any race are rough and turbulent, and it struck Alf that to be out at midnight on a pier-end with such a crowd of wharfmen, in a big Japanese city, was not as safe as it might be.

One burly fellow, with a shock of black hair and ferocious eyes, came up. The rest shoved in after him to take part in the discussion.

"Give me shoes," the man said. "Give me shoes now. I take you 'Merican schooner."

Alf shook his head, whereat the crowd clamored that he accept the proposal. Now the Anglo-Saxon is so constituted that to browbeat or bully him is the last way under the sun of getting him to do any certain thing.

He will dare willingly, but he will not permit himself to be driven. So this attempt of the boatmen to force Alf only aroused all the dogged stubbornness of his race. The same qualities were in him that are in men who lead forlorn hopes; and there, under the stars, on the lonely pier, encircled by the jostling and shouldering gang, he resolved that he would die rather than submit to the indignity of being robbed of a single stitch of clothing. Not value, but principle, was at stake.

Then somebody thrust roughly against him from behind. He whirled about with flashing eyes, and the circle involuntarily gave ground. But the crowd was growing more boisterous. Each and every article of clothing he had on was demanded by one or another, and these demands were shouted simultaneously at the tops of very healthy lungs.

Alf had long since ceased to say anything, but he knew that the situation was getting dangerous, and that the only thing left to him was to get away. His face was set doggedly, his eyes glinted like points of steel, and his body was firmly and confidently poised. This air of determination sufficiently impressed the boatmen to make them give way before him when he started to walk toward the shore-end of the pier. But they trooped along beside him and behind him, shouting and laughing more noisily than ever. One of the youngsters, about Alf's size and build, impudently snatched his cap from his head; but before he could put it on his own head, Alf struck out from the shoulder, and sent the fellow rolling on the stones.

The cap flew out of his hand and disappeared among the many legs. Alf did some quick thinking; his sailor pride would not permit him to leave the cap in their hands. He followed in the direction it had sped, and soon found it under the bare foot of a stalwart fellow, who kept his weight stolidly upon it. Alf tried to get the cap out by a sudden jerk, but failed. He shoved against the man's leg, but the man only grunted. It was challenge direct, and Alf accepted it. Like a flash one leg was behind the man and Alf had thrust strongly with his shoulder against the fellow's chest. Nothing could save the man from the fierce vigorousness of the trick, and he was hurled over and backward.

Next, the cap was on Alf's head and his fists were up before him. Then he whirled about to prevent attack from behind, and all those in that quarter fled precipitately. This was what he wanted. None remained between him and the shore end. The pier was narrow. Facing them and threatening with his fist those who attempted to pass him on either side, he continued his retreat. It was exciting work, walking backward and at the same time checking that surging mass of men. But the dark-skinned peoples, the world over, have learned to respect the white man's fist; and it was the battles fought by many sailors, more than his own warlike front, that gave Alf the victory.

Where the pier adjoins the shore was the station of the harbor police, and Alf backed into the electric-lighted office, very much to the amusement of the dapper lieutenant in charge. The sampan men, grown quiet and orderly, clustered like flies by the open door, through which they could see and hear what passed.

Alf explained his difficulty in few words, and demanded, as the privilege of a stranger in a strange land, that the lieutenant put him aboard in the police-boat. The lieutenant, in turn, who knew all the "rules and regulations" by heart, explained that the harbor police were not ferrymen, and that the police-boats had other functions to perform than that of transporting belated and penniless sailor-men to their ships. He also said he knew the sampan men to be natural-born robbers, but that so long as they robbed within the law he was powerless. It was their right to collect fares in advance, and who was he to command them to take a passenger and collect fare at the journey's end? Alf acknowledged the justice of his remarks, but suggested that while he could not command he might persuade. The lieutenant was willing to oblige, and went to the door, from where he delivered a speech to the crowd. But they, too, knew their rights, and, when the officer had finished, shouted in chorus their abominable "Ten sen! You pay now! You pay now!"

"You see, I can do nothing," said the lieutenant, who, by the way, spoke perfect English. "But I have warned them not to harm or molest you, so you will be safe, at least. The night is warm and half over. Lie down somewhere and go to sleep. I would permit you to sleep here in the office, were it not against the rules and regulations."

Alf thanked him for his kindness and courtesy; but the sampan men had aroused all his pride of race and doggedness, and the problem could not be solved that way. To sleep out the night on the stones was an acknowledgment of defeat.

"The sampan men refuse to take me out?"

The lieutenant nodded.

"And you refuse to take me out?"

Again the lieutenant nodded.

"Well, then, it's not in the rules and regulations that you can prevent my taking myself out?"

The lieutenant was perplexed. "There is no boat," he said.

"That's not the question," Alf proclaimed hotly. "If I take myself out, everybody's satisfied and no harm done?"

"Yes; what you say is true," persisted the puzzled lieutenant. "But you cannot take yourself out."

"You just watch me," was the retort.

Down went Alf's cap on the office floor. Right and left he kicked off his low-cut shoes. Trousers and shirt followed.

"Remember," he said in ringing tones, "I, as a citizen of the United States, shall hold you, the city of Yokohama, and the government of Japan responsible for those clothes. Good night."

He plunged through the doorway, scattering the astounded boatmen to either side, and ran out on the pier. But they quickly recovered and ran after him, shouting with glee at the new phase the situation had taken on. It was a night long remembered among the water-folk of Yokohama town. Straight to the end Alf ran, and, without pause, dived off cleanly and neatly into the water. He struck out with a lusty, single-overhand stroke till curiosity prompted him to halt for a moment. Out of the darkness, from where the pier should be, voices were calling to him.

He turned on his back, floated, and listened.

"All right! All right!" he could distinguish from the babel. "No pay now; pay bime by! Come back! Come back now; pay bime by!"

"No, thank you," he called back. "No pay at all. Good night."

Then he faced about in order to locate the Annie Mine. She was fully a mile away, and in the darkness it was no easy task to get her bearings. First, he settled upon a blaze of lights which he knew nothing but a man-of-war could make. That must be the United States war-ship Lancaster. Somewhere to the left and beyond should be the Annie Mine. But to the left he made out three lights close together. That could not be the schooner. For the moment he was confused. He rolled over on his back and shut his eyes, striving to construct a mental picture of the harbor as he had seen it in daytime. With a snort of satisfaction he rolled back again. The three lights evidently belonged to the big English tramp steamer. Therefore the schooner must lie somewhere between the three lights and the Lancaster. He gazed long and steadily, and there, very dim and low, but at the point he expected, burned a single light— the anchor-light of the Annie Mine.

And it was a fine swim under the starshine. The air was warm as the water, and the water as warm as tepid milk. The good salt taste of it was in his mouth, the tingling of it along his limbs; and the steady beat of his heart, heavy and strong, made him glad for living.

But beyond being glorious the swim was uneventful. On the right hand he passed the many-lighted Lancaster, on the left hand the English tramp, and ere long the Annie Mine loomed large above him. He grasped the hanging rope-ladder and drew himself noiselessly on deck. There was no one in sight. He saw a light in the galley, and knew that the captain's son, who kept the lonely anchor-watch, was making coffee. Alf went forward to the forecastle. The men were snoring in their bunks, and in that confined space the heat seemed to him insufferable. So he put on a thin cotton shirt and a pair of dungaree trousers, tucked blanket and pillow under his arm, and went up on deck and out on the fore-castle-head.

Hardly had he begun to doze when he was roused by a boat coming alongside and hailing the anchor-watch. It was the police-boat, and to Alf it was given to enjoy the excited conversation that ensued. Yes, the captain's son recognized the clothes. They belonged to Alf Davis, one of the seamen. What had happened? No; Alf Davis had not come aboard. He was ashore. He was not ashore? Then he must be drowned. Here both the lieutenant and the captain's son talked at the same time, and Alf could make out nothing. Then he heard them come forward and rouse out the crew. The crew grumbled sleepily and said that Alf Davis was not in the forecastle; whereupon the captain's son waxed indignant at the Yokohama police and their ways, and the lieutenant quoted rules and regulations in despairing accents.

Alf rose up from the forecastle-head and extended his hand, saying:

"I guess I'll take those clothes. Thank you for bringing them aboard so promptly."

"I don't see why he couldn't have brought you aboard inside of them," said the captain's son.

And the police lieutenant said nothing, though he turned the clothes over somewhat sheepishly to their rightful owner.

The next day, when Alf started to go ashore, he found himself surrounded by shouting and gesticulating, though very respectful, sampan men, all extraordinarily anxious to have him for a passenger. Nor did the one he selected say, "You pay now," when he entered his boat. When Alf prepared to step out on to the pier, he offered the man the customary ten sen. But the man drew himself up and shook his head.

"You all right," he said. "You no pay. You never no pay. You bully boy and all right."

And for the rest of the Annie Mine's stay in port, the sampan men refused money at Alf Davis's hand. Out of admiration for his pluck and independence, they had given him the freedom of the harbor.

WHOSE BUSINESS IS TO LIVE

Stanton Davies and Jim Wemple ceased from their talk to listen to an increase of uproar in the street. A volley of stones thrummed and boomed the wire mosquito nettings that protected the windows. It was a hot night, and the sweat of the heat stood on their faces as they listened. Arose the incoherent clamor of the mob, punctuated by individual cries in Mexican-Spanish. Least terrible among the obscene threats were: "Death to the Gringos!" "Kill the American pigs!" "Drown the American dogs in the sea!"

Stanton Davies and Jim Wemple shrugged their shoulders patiently to each other, and resumed their conversation, talking louder in order to make themselves heard above the uproar.

"The question is how," Wemple said. "It's forty-seven miles to Panuco, by river——"

"And the land's impossible, with Zaragoza's and Villa's men on the loot and maybe fraternizing," Davies agreed.

Wemple nodded and continued: "And she's at the East Coast Magnolia, two miles beyond, if she isn't back at the hunting camp. We've got to get her——"

"We've played pretty square in this matter, Wemple," Davies said. "And we might as well speak up and acknowledge what each of us knows the other knows. You want her. I want her."

Wemple lighted a cigarette and nodded.

"And now's the time when it's up to us to make a show as if we didn't want her and that all we want is just to save her and get her down here."

"And a truce until we do save her—I get you," Wempel affirmed.

"A truce until we get her safe and sound back here in Tampico, or aboard a battleship. After that? ..."

Both men shrugged shoulders and beamed on each other as their hands met in ratification.

Fresh volleys of stones thrummed against the wire-screened windows; a boy's voice rose shrilly above the clamor, proclaiming death to the Gringos; and the house reverberated to the heavy crash of some battering ram against the street-door downstairs. Both men, snatching up automatic rifles, ran down to where their fire could command the threatened door.

"If they break in we've got to let them have it," Wemple said.

Davies nodded quiet agreement, then inconsistently burst out with a lurid string of oaths.

"To think of it!" he explained his wrath. "One out of three of those curs outside has worked for you or me—lean-bellied, barefooted, poverty-stricken, glad for ten centavos a day if they could only get work. And we've given them steady jobs and a hundred and fifty centavos a day, and here they are yelling for our blood."

"Only the half breeds," Davies corrected.

"You know what I mean," Wemple replied. "The only peons we've lost are those that have been run off or shot."

The attack on the door ceasing, they returned upstairs. Half a dozen scattered shots from farther along the street seemed to draw away the mob, for the neighborhood became comparatively quiet.

A whistle came to them through the open windows, and a man's voice calling:

"Wemple! Open the door! It's Habert! Want to talk to you!"

Wemple went down, returning in several minutes with a tidily-paunched, well-built, gray-haired American of fifty. He shook hands with Davies and flung himself into a chair, breathing heavily. He did not relinquish his clutch on the Colt's 44 automatic pistol, although he immediately addressed himself to the task of fishing a filled clip of cartridges from the pocket of his linen coat. He had arrived hatless and breathless, and the blood from a stone-cut on the cheek oozed down his face. He, too, in a fit of anger, springing to his feet when he had changed clips in his pistol, burst out with mouth-filling profanity.

"They had an American flag in the dirt, stamping and spitting on it. And they told me to spit on it."

Wemple and Davies regarded him with silent interrogation.

"Oh, I know what you're wondering!" he flared out. "Would I a-spit on it in the pinch? That's what's eating you. I'll answer. Straight out, brass tacks, I WOULD. Put that in your pipe and smoke it."

He paused to help himself to a cigar from the box on the table and to light it with a steady and defiant hand.

"Hell!—I guess this neck of the woods knows Anthony Habert, and you can bank on it that it's never located his yellow streak. Sure, in the pinch, I'd spit on Old Glory. What the hell d'ye think I'm going on the streets for a night like this? Didn't I skin out of the Southern Hotel half an hour ago, where there are forty buck Americans, not counting their women, and all armed? That was safety. What d'ye think I came here for?—to rescue you?"

His indignation lumped his throat into silence, and he seemed shaken as with an apoplexy.

"Spit it out," Davies commanded dryly.

"I'll tell you," Habert exploded. "It's Billy Boy. Fifty miles up country and twenty-thousand throat-cutting federals and rebels between him and me. D'ye know what that boy'd do, if he was here in Tampico and I was fifty miles up the Panuco? Well, I know. And I'm going to do the same—go and get him."

"We're figuring on going up," Wemple assured him.

"And that's why I headed here—Miss Drexel, of course?"

Both men acquiesced and smiled. It was a time when men dared speak of matters which at other times tabooed speech.

"Then the thing's to get started," Habert exclaimed, looking at his watch. "It's midnight now. We've got to get to the river and get a boat—"

But the clamor of the returning mob came through the windows in answer.

Davies was about to speak, when the telephone rang, and Wemple sprang to the instrument.

"It's Carson," he interjected, as he listened. "They haven't cut the wires across the river yet.—Hello, Carson. Was it a break or a cut? ... Bully for you.... Yes, move the mules across to the potrero beyond Tamcochin.... Who's at the water station? ... Can you still 'phone him? ... Tell him to keep the tanks full, and to shut off the main to Arico. Also, to hang on till the last minute, and keep a horse saddled to cut and run for it. Last thing before he runs, he must jerk out the 'phone.... Yes, yes, yes. Sure. No breeds. Leave full-blooded Indians in charge. Gabriel is a good hombre. Heaven knows, once we're chased out, when we'll get back.... You can't pinch down Jaramillo under twenty-five hundred barrels. We've got storage for ten days. Gabriel'll have to handle it. Keep it moving, if we have to run it into the river——"

"Ask him if he has a launch," Habert broke in.

"He hasn't," was Wemple's answer. "The federals commandeered the last one at noon."

"Say, Carson, how are you going to make your get-away?" Wemple queried.

The man to whom he talked was across the Panuco, on the south side, at the tank farm.

"Says there isn't any get-away," Wemple vouchsafed to the other two. "The federals are all over the shop, and he can't understand why they haven't raided him hours ago."

"... Who? Campos? That skunk! ... all right.... Don't be worried if you don't hear from me. I'm going up river with Davies and Habert.... Use your judgment, and if you get a safe chance at Campos, pot him.... Oh, a hot time over here. They're battering our doors now. Yes, by all means ... Good-by, old man."

Wemple lighted a cigarette and wiped his forehead.

"You know Campos, José H. Campos," he volunteered. "The dirty cur's stuck Carson up for twenty thousand pesos. We had to pay, or he'd have compelled half our peons to enlist or set the wells on fire. And you know, Davies, what we've done for him in past years. Gratitude? Simple decency? Great Scott!"

It was the night of April twenty-first. On the morning of the twenty-first the American marines and bluejackets had landed at Vera Cruz and seized the custom house and the city. Immediately the news was telegraphed, the vengeful Mexican mob had taken possession of the streets of Tampico and expressed its disapproval of the action of the United States by tearing down American flags and crying death to the Americans.

There was nothing save its own spinelessness to deter the mob from carrying out its threat. Had it battered down the doors of the Southern Hotel, or of other hotels, or of residences such as Wemple's, a fight would have started in which the thousands of federal soldiers in Tampico would have joined their civilian compatriots in the laudable task of decreasing the Gringo population of that particular portion of Mexico. There should have been American warships to act as deterrents; but through some inexplicable excess of delicacy, or strategy, or heaven knows what, the United States, when it gave its orders to take Vera Cruz, had very carefully withdrawn its warships from Tampico to the open Gulf a dozen miles away. This order had come to Admiral Mayo by wireless from Washington, and thrice he had demanded the order to be repeated, ere, with tears in his eyes, he had turned his back on his countrymen and countrywomen and steamed to sea.

"Of all asinine things, to leave us in the lurch this way!" Habert was denouncing the powers that be of his country. "Mayo'd never have done it. Mark my words, he had to take program from Washington. And here we are,

85

and our dear ones scattered for fifty miles back up country.... Say, if I lose Billy Boy I'll never dare go home to face the wife.—Come on. Let the three of us make a start. We can throw the fear of God into any gang on the streets."

"Come on over and take a squint," Davies invited from where he stood, somewhat back from the window, looking down into the street.

It was gorged with rioters, all haranguing, cursing, crying out death, and urging one another to smash the doors, but each hanging back from the death he knew waited behind those doors for the first of the rush.

"We can't break through a bunch like that, Habert," was Davies' comment.

"And if we die under their feet we'll be of little use to Billy Boy or anybody else up the Panuco," Wemple added. "And if——"

A new movement of the mob caused him to break off. It was splitting before a slow and silent advance of a file of white-clad men.

"Bluejackets—Mayo's come back for us after all," Habert muttered.

"Then we can get a navy launch," Davies said.

The bedlam of the mob died away, and, in silence, the sailors reached the street door and knocked for admittance. All three went down to open it, and to discover that the callers were not Americans but two German lieutenants and half a dozen German marines. At sight of the Americans, the rage of the mob rose again, and was quelled by the grounding of the rifle butts of the marines.

"No, thank you," the senior lieutenant, in passable English, declined the invitation to enter. He unconcernedly kept his cigar alive at such times that the mob drowned his voice. "We are on the way back to our ship. Our commander conferred with the English and Dutch commanders; but they declined to cooperate, so our commander has undertaken the entire responsibility. We have been the round of the hotels. They are to hold their own until daybreak, when we'll take them off. We have given them rockets such as these.—Take them. If your house is entered, hold your own and send up a rocket from the roof. We can be here in force, in forty-five minutes. Steam is up in all our launches, launch crews and marines for shore duty are in the launches, and at the first rocket we shall start."

"Since you are going aboard now, we should like to go with you," Davies said, after having rendered due thanks.

The surprise and distaste on both lieutenants' faces was patent.

"Oh, no," Davies laughed. "We don't want refuge. We have friends fifty miles up river, and we want to get to the river in order to go up after them."

The pleasure on the officers' faces was immediate as they looked a silent conference at each other.

"Since our commander has undertaken grave responsibility on a night like this, may we do less than take minor responsibility?" queried the elder.

To this the younger heartily agreed. In a trice, upstairs and down again, equipped with extra ammunition, extra pistols, and a pocket-bulging supply of cigars, cigarettes and matches, the three Americans were ready. Wemple called last instructions up the stairway to imaginary occupants being left behind, ascertained that the spring lock was on, and slammed the door.

The officers led, followed by the Americans, the rear brought up by the six marines; and the spitting, howling mob, not daring to cast a stone, gave way before them.

As they came alongside the gangway of the cruiser, they saw launches and barges lying in strings to the boat-booms, filled with men, waiting for the rocket signal from the beleaguered hotels. A gun thundered from close at hand, up river, followed by the thunder of numerous guns and the reports of many rifles fired very rapidly.

"Now what's the Topila whanging away at?" Habert complained, then joined the others in gazing at the picture.

A searchlight, evidently emanating from the Mexican gunboat, was stabbing the darkness to the middle of the river, where it played upon the water. And across the water, the center of the moving circle of light, flashed a long, lean speedboat. A shell burst in the air a hundred feet astern of it. Somewhere, outside the light, other shells were bursting in the water; for they saw the boat rocked by the waves from the explosions. They could guess the whizzing of the rifle bullets.

But for only several minutes the spectacle lasted. Such was the speed of the boat that it gained shelter behind the German, when the Mexican gunboat was compelled to cease fire. The speedboat slowed down, turned in a wide and heeling circle, and ranged up alongside the launch at the gangway.

The lights from the gangway showed but one occupant, a tow-headed, greasy-faced, blond youth of twenty, very lean, very calm, very much satisfied with himself.

"If it ain't Peter Tonsburg!" Habert ejaculated, reaching out a hand to shake. "Howdy, Peter, howdy. And where in hell are you hellbent for, surging by the Topila in such scandalous fashion!"

Peter, a Texas-born Swede of immigrant parents, filled with the old Texas traditions, greasily shook hands with Wemple and Davies as well, saying "Howdy," as only the Texan born can say it.

"Me," he answered Habert. "I ain't hellbent nowhere exceptin' to get away from the shell-fire. She's a caution, that Topila. Huh! but I limbered 'em up some. I was goin' every inch of twenty-five. They was like amateurs blazin' away at canvasback."

"Which Chill is it?" Wemple asked.

"Chill II," Peter answered. "It's all that's left. Chill I a Greaser—you know 'm—Campos—commandeered this noon. I was runnin' Chill III when they caught me at sundown. Made me come in under their guns at the East Coast outfit, and fired me out on my neck.

"Now the boss'd gone over in this one to Tampico in the early evening, and just about ten minutes ago I spots it landin' with a sousy bunch of Federals at the East Coast, and swipes it back according. Where's the boss?

88

He ain't hurt, is he? Because I'm going after him."

"No, you're not, Peter," Davies said. "Mr. Frisbie is safe at the Southern Hotel, all except a five-inch scalp wound from a brick that's got him down with a splitting headache. He's safe, so you're going with us, going to take us, I mean, up beyond Panuco town."

"Huh?—I can see myself," Peter retorted, wiping his greasy nose on a wad of greasy cotton waste. "I got some cold. Besides, this night-drivin' ain't good for my complexion."

"My boy's up there," Habert said.

"Well, he's bigger'n I am, and I reckon he can take care of himself."

"And there's a woman there—Miss Drexel," Davies said quietly.

"Who? Miss Drexel? Why didn't you say so at first!" Peter demanded grievedly. He sighed and added, "Well, climb in an' make a start. Better get your Dutch friends to donate me about twenty gallons of gasoline if you want to get anywhere."

"Won't do you no good to lay low," Peter Tonsburg remarked, as, at full speed, headed up river, the Topila's searchlight stabbed them. "High or low, if one of them shells hits in the vicinity—good night!"

Immediately thereafter the Topila erupted. The roar of the Chill's exhaust nearly drowned the roar of the guns, but the fragile hull of the craft was shaken and rocked by the bursting shells. An occasional bullet thudded into or pinged off the Chill, and, despite Peter's warning that, high or low, they were bound to get it if it came to them, every man on board, including Peter, crouched, with chest contracted by drawn-in shoulders, in an instinctive and purely unconscious effort to lessen the area of body he presented as a target or receptacle for flying fragments of steel.

The Topila was a federal gunboat. To complicate the affair, the constitutionalists, gathered on the north shore in the siege of Tampico, opened up on the speedboat with many rifles and a machine gun.

"Lord, I'm glad they're Mexicans, and not Americans," Habert observed, after five mad minutes in which no damage had been received. "Mexicans are born with guns in their hands, and they never learn to use them."

Nor was the Chill or any man aboard damaged when at last she rounded the bend of river that shielded her from the searchlight.

"I'll have you in Panuco town in less'n three hours, ... if we don't hit a log," Peter leaned back and shouted in Wemple's ear. "And if we do hit driftwood, I'll have you in the swim quicker than that."

Chill II tore her way through the darkness, steered by the tow-headed youth who knew every foot of the river and who guided his course by the loom of the banks in the dim starlight. A smart breeze, kicking up spiteful wavelets on the wider reaches, splashed them with sheeted water as well as fine-flung spray. And, in the face of the warmth of the tropic night, the wind, added to the speed of the boat, chilled them through their wet clothes.

"Now I know why she was named the Chill," Habert observed betwixt chattering teeth.

But conversation languished during the nearly three hours of drive through the darkness. Once, by the exhaust, they knew that they passed an unlighted launch bound down stream. And once, a glare of light, near the south bank, as they passed through the Toreno field, aroused brief debate as to whether it was the Toreno wells, or the bungalow on Merrick's banana plantation that flared so fiercely.

At the end of an hour, Peter slowed down and ran in to the bank.

"I got a cache of gasoline here—ten gallons," he explained, "and it's just as well to know it's here for the back trip." Without leaving the boat, fishing arm-deep into the brush, he announced, "All hunky-dory." He proceeded to oil the engine. "Huh!" he soliloquized for their benefit. "I was just readin' a magazine yarn last night. 'Whose Business Is to Die,' was its title. An' all I got to say is, 'The hell it is.' A man's business is to live. Maybe you thought it was our business to die when the Topila was pepper-in' us. But you was wrong. We're alive, ain't we? We beat her to it. That's the game. Nobody's got any business to die. I ain't never goin' to die, if I've got any say about it."

He turned over the crank, and the roar and rush of the Chill put an end to speech.

There was no need for Wemple or Davies to speak further in the affair closest to their hearts. Their truce to love-making had been made as binding as it was brief, and each rival honored the other with a firm belief that he would commit no infraction of the truce. Afterward was another matter. In the meantime they were one in the effort to get Beth Drexel back to the safety of riotous Tampico or of a war vessel.

It was four o'clock when they passed by Panuco Town. Shouts and songs told them that the federal detachment holding the place was celebrating its indignation at the landing of American bluejackets in Vera Cruz. Sentinels challenged the Chill from the shore and shot at random at the noise of her in the darkness.

A mile beyond, where a lighted river steamer with steam up lay at the north bank, they ran in at the Apshodel wells. The steamer was small, and the nearly two hundred Americans—men, women, and children—crowded her capacity. Blasphemous greetings of pure joy and geniality were exchanged between the men, and Habert learned that the steamboat was waiting for his Billy Boy, who, astride a horse, was rounding up isolated drilling gangs who had not yet learned that the United States had seized Vera Cruz and that all Mexico was boiling.

Habert climbed out to wait and to go down on the steamer, while the three that remained on the Chill, having learned that Miss Drexel was not with the refugees, headed for the Dutch Company on the south shore. This was the big gusher, pinched down from one hundred and eighty-five thousand daily barrels to the quantity the company was able to handle. Mexico had no quarrel with Holland, so that the superintendent, while up, with night guards out to prevent drunken soldiers from firing his vast lakes of oil, was quite unemotional. Yes, the last he had heard was that Miss Drexel and her brother were back at the hunting lodge. No; he had not sent any warnings, and he doubted that anybody else had. Not till ten o'clock the previous evening had he learned of the landing at Vera Cruz. The Mexicans had turned nasty as soon as they heard of it, and they had killed Miles Forman at the Empire Wells, run off his labor, and looted the camp. Horses? No; he didn't have horse or mule on the place. The federals had commandeered the last animal weeks back. It was his belief, however, that there were a couple of plugs at the lodge, too worthless even for the Mexicans to take.

"It's a hike," Davies said cheerfully.

"Six miles of it," Wemple agreed, equally cheerfully. "Let's beat it."

A shot from the river, where they had left Peter in the boat, started them on the run for the bank. A scattering of shots, as from two rifles, followed. And while the Dutch superintendent, in execrable Spanish, shouted affirmations of Dutch neutrality into the menacing dark, across the gunwale of Chill II they found the body of the tow-headed youth whose business it had been not to die.

For the first hour, talking little, Davies and Wemple stumbled along the apology for a road that led through the jungle to the lodge. They did discuss the glares of several fires to the east along the south bank of Panuco River, and hoped fervently that they were dwellings and not wells.

"Two billion dollars worth of oil right here in the Ebaño field alone," Davies grumbled.

"And a drunken Mexican, whose whole carcass and immortal soul aren't worth ten pesos including hair, hide, and tallow, can start the bonfire with a lighted wad of cotton waste," was Wemple's contribution. "And if ever she starts, she'll gut the field of its last barrel."

Dawn, at five, enabled them to accelerate their pace; and six o'clock found them routing out the occupants of the lodge.

"Dress for rough travel, and don't stop for any frills," Wemple called around the corner of Miss Drexel's screened sleeping porch.

"Not a wash, nothing," Davies supplemented grimly, as he shook hands with Charley Drexel, who yawned and slippered up to them in pajamas. "Where are those horses, Charley? Still alive?"

Wemple finished giving orders to the sleepy peons to remain and care for the place, occupying their spare time with hiding the more valuable things, and was calling around the corner to Miss Drexel the news of the capture of Vera Cruz, when Davies returned with the information that the horses consisted of a pair of moth-eaten skates that could be depended upon to lie down and die in the first half mile.

Beth Drexel emerged, first protesting that under no circumstances would she be guilty of riding the creatures, and, next, her brunette skin and dark eyes still flushed warm with sleep, greeting the two rescuers.

"It would be just as well if you washed your face, Stanton," she told Davies; and, to Wemple: "You're just as bad, Jim. You are a pair of dirty boys."

"And so will you be," Wemple assured her, "before you get back to Tampico. Are you ready?"

"As soon as Juanita packs my hand bag."

"Heavens, Beth, don't waste time!" exclaimed Wemple. "Jump in and grab up what you want."

"Make a start—make a start," chanted Davies. "Hustle! Hustle!—Charley, get the rifle you like best and take it along. Get a couple for us."

"Is it as serious as that?" Miss Drexel queried.

Both men nodded.

"The Mexicans are tearing loose," Davies explained. "How they missed this place I don't know." A movement in the adjoining room startled him. "Who's that?" he cried.

"Why, Mrs. Morgan," Miss Drexel answered.

"Good heavens, Wemple, I'd forgotten her," groaned Davies. "How will we ever get her anywhere?"

"Let Beth walk, and relay the lady on the nags."

"She weighs a hundred and eighty," Miss Drexel laughed. "Oh, hurry,

Martha! We're waiting on you to start!"

Muffled speech came through the partition, and then emerged a very short, stout, much-flustered woman of middle age.

"I simply can't walk, and you boys needn't demand it of me," was her plaint. "It's no use. I couldn't walk half a mile to save my life, and it's six of the worst miles to the river."

They regarded her in despair.

"Then you'll ride," said Davies. "Come on, Charley. We'll get a saddle on each of the nags."

Along the road through the tropic jungle, Miss Drexel and Juanita, her Indian maid, led the way. Her brother, carrying the three rifles, brought up the rear, while in the middle Davies and Wemple struggled with Mrs. Morgan and the two decrepit steeds. One, a flea-bitten roan, groaned continually from the moment Mrs. Morgan's burden was put upon him till she was shifted to the other horse. And this other, a mangy sorrel, invariably lay down at the end of a quarter of a mile of Mrs. Morgan.

Miss Drexel laughed and joked and encouraged; and Wemple, in brutal fashion, compelled Mrs. Morgan to walk every third quarter of a mile. At the end of an hour the sorrel refused positively to get up, and, so, was abandoned. Thereafter, Mrs. Morgan rode the roan alternate quarters of miles, and between times walked—if walk may describe her stumbling progress on two preposterously tiny feet with a man supporting her on either side.

A mile from the river, the road became more civilized, running along the side of a thousand acres of banana plantation.

"Parslow's," young Drexel said. "He'll lose a year's crop now on account of this mix-up."

"Oh, look what I've found!" Miss Drexel called from the lead.

"First machine that ever tackled this road," was young Drexel's judgment, as they halted to stare at the tire-tracks.

"But look at the tracks," his sister urged. "The machine must have come right out of the bananas and climbed the bank."

"Some machine to climb a bank like that," was Davies' comment. "What it did do was to go down the bank—take a scout after it, Charley, while Wemple and I get Mrs. Morgan off her fractious mount. No machine ever built could travel far through those bananas."

The flea-bitten roan, on its four legs upstanding, continued bravely to stand until the lady was removed, whereupon, with a long sigh, it sank down on the ground. Mrs. Morgan likewise sighed, sat down, and regarded her tiny feet mournfully.

"Go on, boys," she said. "Maybe you can find something at the river and send back for me."

But their indignant rejection of the plan never attained speech, for, at that instant, from the green sea of banana trees beneath them, came the sudden purr of an engine. A minute later the splutter of an exhaust told them the silencer had been taken off. The huge-fronded banana trees were violently agitated as by the threshing of a hidden Titan. They could identify the changing of gears and the reversing and going ahead, until, at the end of five minutes, a long low, black car burst from the wall of greenery and charged the soft earth bank, but the earth was too soft, and when, two-thirds of the way up, beaten, Charley Drexel braked the car to a standstill, the earth crumbled from under the tires, and he ran it down and back, the way he had come, until half-buried in the bananas.

"'A Merry Oldsmobile!'" Miss Drexel quoted from the popular song, clapping her hands. "Now, Martha, your troubles are over."

"Six-cylinder, and sounds as if it hadn't been out of the shop a week, or may I never ride in a machine again," Wemple remarked, looking to Davies for confirmation.

Davies nodded.

"It's Allison's," he said. "Campos tried to shake him down for a private loan, and—well, you know Allison. He told Campos to go to. And Campos, in revenge, commandeered his new car. That was two days ago, before we lifted a hand at Vera Cruz. Allison told me yesterday the last he'd heard of the car it was on a steamboat bound up river. And here's where they ditched it—but let's get a hustle on and get her into the running."

Three attempts they made, with young Drexel at the wheel; but the soft earth and the pitch of the grade baffled.

"She's got the power all right," young Drexel protested. "But she can't bite into that mush."

So far, they had spread on the ground the robes found in the car. The men now added their coats, and Wemple, for additional traction, unsaddled the roan, and spread the cinches, stirrup leathers, saddle blanket, and bridle in the way of the wheels. The car took the treacherous slope in a rush, with churning wheels biting into the woven fabrics; and, with no more than a hint of hesitation, it cleared the crest and swung into the road.

"Isn't she the spunky devil!" Drexel exulted. "Say, she could climb the side of a house if she could get traction."

"Better put on that silencer again, if you don't want to play tag with every soldier in the district," Wemple ordered, as they helped Mrs. Morgan in.

The road to the Dutch gusher compelled them to go through the outskirts of Panuco town. Indian and half breed women gazed stolidly at the strange vehicle, while the children and barking dogs clamorously advertised its progress. Once, passing long lines of tethered federal horses, they were challenged by a sentry; but at Wemple's "Throw on the juice!" the car took the rutted road at fifty miles an hour. A shot whistled after them. But it was not the shot that made Mrs. Morgan scream. The cause was a series of hog-wallows masked with mud, which nearly tore the steering wheel from Drexel's hands before he could reduce speed.

"Wonder it didn't break an axle," Davies growled. "Go on and take it easy, Charley. We're past any interference."

They swung into the Dutch camp and into the beginning of their real troubles. The refugee steamboat had departed down river from the Asphodel camp; Chill II had disappeared, the superintendent knew not how, along with the body of Peter Tonsburg; and the superintendent was dubious of their remaining.

"I've got to consider the owners," he told them. "This is the biggest well in Mexico, and you know it—a hundred and eighty-five thousand barrels daily flow. I've no right to risk it. We have no trouble with the Mexicans. It's you Americans. If you stay here, I'll have to protect you. And I can't protect you, anyway. We'll all lose our lives and they'll destroy the well in the bargain. And if they fire it, it means the entire Ebaño oil field. The strata's too broken. We're flowing twenty thousand barrels now, and we can't pinch down any further. As it is, the oil's coming up outside the pipe. And we can't have a fight. We've got to keep the oil moving."

The men nodded. It was cold-blooded logic; but there was no fault to it.

The harassed expression eased on the superintendent's face, and he almost beamed on them for agreeing with him.

"You've got a good machine there," he continued. "The ferry's at the bank at Panuco, and once you're across, the rebels aren't so thick on the north shore. Why, you can beat the steamboat back to Tampico by hours. And it hasn't rained for days. The road won't be at all bad."

"Which is all very good," Davies observed to Wemple as they approached Panuco, "except for the fact that the road on the other side was never built for automobiles, much less for a long-bodied one like this. I wish it were the Four instead of the Six."

"And it would bother you with a Four to negotiate that hill at Aliso where the road switchbacks above the river."

"And we're going to do it with a Six or lose a perfectly good Six in trying," Beth Drexel laughed to them.

Avoiding the cavalry camp, they entered Panuco with all the speed the ruts permitted, swinging dizzy corners to the squawking of chickens and barking of dogs. To gain the ferry, they had to pass down one side of the great plaza which was the heart of the city. Peon soldiers, drowsing in the sun or clustering around the cantinas, stared stupidly at them as they flashed past. Then a drunken major shouted a challenge from the doorway of a cantina and began vociferating orders, and as they left the plaza behind they could hear rising the familiar mob-cry "Kill the Gringoes!"

"If any shooting begins, you women get down in the bottom of the car," Davies commanded. "And there's the ferry all right. Be careful, Charley."

The machine plunged directly down the bank through a cut so deep that it was more like a chute, struck the gangplank with a terrific bump, and seemed fairly to leap on board. The ferry was scarcely longer than the machine, and Drexel, visibly shaken by the closeness of the shave, managed to stop only when six inches remained between the front wheels and overboard.

It was a cable ferry, operated by gasoline, and, while Wemple cast off the mooring lines, Davies was making swift acquaintance with the engine. The third turn-over started it, and he threw it into gear with the windlass that began winding up the cable from the river's bottom.

By the time they were in midstream a score of horsemen rode out on the bank they had just left and opened a scattering fire. The party crowded in the shelter of the car and listened to the occasional richochet of a bullet. Once, only, the car was struck.

"Here!—what are you up to!" Wemple demanded suddenly of Drexel, who had exposed himself to fish a rifle out of the car.

"Going to show the skunks what shooting is," was his answer.

"No, you don't," Wemple said. "We're not here to fight, but to get this party to Tampico." He remembered Peter Tonsburg's remark. "Whose business is to live, Charley—that's our business. Anybody can get killed. It's too easy these days."

Still under fire, they moored at the north shore, and when Davies had tossed overboard the igniter from the ferry engine and commandeered ten gallons of its surplus gasoline, they took the steep, soft road up the bank in a rush.

"Look at her climb," Drexel uttered gleefully. "That Aliso hill won't bother us at all. She'll put a crimp in it, that's what she'll do."

"It isn't the hill, it's the sharp turn of the zig-zag that's liable to put a crimp in her," Davies answered. "That road was never laid out for autos, and no auto has ever been over it. They steamboated this one up."

But trouble came before Aliso was reached. Where the road dipped abruptly into a small jag of hollow that was almost V-shaped, it arose out and became a hundred yards of deep sand. In order to have speed left for the sand after he cleared the stiff up-grade of the V, Drexel was compelled to hit the trough of the V with speed. Wemple clutched Miss Drexel as she was on the verge of being bounced out. Mrs. Morgan, too solid for such airiness, screamed from the pain of the bump; and even the imperturbable Juanita fell to crossing herself and uttering prayers with exceeding rapidity.

The car cleared the crest and encountered the sand, going slower from moment to moment, slewing and writhing and squirming from side to side. The men leaped out and began shoving. Miss Drexel urged Juanita out and followed. But the car came to a standstill, and Drexel, looking back and pointing, showed the first sign of being beaten. Two things he pointed to: a constitutional soldier on horseback a quarter of a mile in the rear; and a portion of the narrow road that had fallen out bodily on the far slope of the V.

"Can't get at this sand unless we go back and try over, and we ditch the car if we try to back up that."

The ditch was a huge natural sump-hole, the stagnant surface of which was a-crawl with slime twenty feet beneath.

Davies and Wemple sprang to take the boy's place.

"You can't do it," he urged. "You can get the back wheels past, but right there you hit that little curve, and if you make it your front wheel will be off the bank. If you don't make it, your back wheel'll be off."

Both men studied it carefully, then looked at each other.

"We've got to," said Davies.

"And we're going to," Wemple said, shoving his rival aside in comradely fashion and taking the post of danger at the wheel. "You're just as good as I at the wheel, Davies," he explained. "But you're a better shot. Your job's cut out to go back and hold off any Greasers that show up."

Davies took a rifle and strolled back with so ominous an air that the lone cavalryman put spurs to his horse and fled. Mrs. Morgan was helped out and sent plodding and tottering unaided on her way to the end of the sand stretch. Miss Drexel and Juanita joined Charley in spreading the coats and robes on the sand and in gathering and spreading small branches, brush, and armfuls of a dry, brittle shrub. But all three ceased from their exertions to watch Wemple as he shot the car backward down the V and up. The car seemed first to stand on one end, then on the other, and to reel drunkenly and to threaten to turn over into the sump-hole when its right front wheel fell into the air where the road had ceased to be. But the hind wheels bit and climbed the grade and out.

Without pause, gathering speed down the perilous slope, Wemple came ahead and up, gaining fifty feet of sand over the previous failure. More of the alluvial soil of the road had dropped out at the bad place; but he took the V in reverse, overhung the front wheel as before, and from the top came ahead again. Four times he did this, gaining each time, but each time knocking a bigger hole where the road fell out, until Miss Drexel begged him not to try again.

He pointed to a squad of horsemen coming at a gallop along the road a mile in the rear, and took the V once again in reverse.

"If only we had more stuff," Drexel groaned to his sister, as he threw down a meager, hard-gathered armful of the dry and brittle shrub, and as Wemple once more, with rush and roar, shot down the V.

For an instant it seemed that the great car would turn over into the sump, but the next instant it was past. It struck the bottom of the hollow a mighty wallop, and bounced and upended to the steep pitch of the climb. Miss Drexel, seized by inspiration or desperation, with a quick movement stripped off her short, corduroy tramping-skirt, and, looking very lithe and boyish in slender-cut pongee bloomers, ran along the sand and dropped the skirt for a foothold for the slowly revolving wheels. Almost, but not quite, did the car stop, then, gathering way, with the others running alongside and shoving, it emerged on the hard road.

While they tossed the robes and coats and Miss Drexel's skirt into the bottom of the car and got Mrs. Morgan on board, Davies overtook them.

"Down on the bottom!—all of you!" he shouted, as he gained the running board and the machine sprang away. A scattering of shots came from the rear.

"Whose business is to live!—hunch down!" Davies yelled in Wemple's ear, accompanying the instruction with an open-handed blow on the shoulder.

"Live yourself," Wemple grumbled as he obediently hunched. "Get your head down. You're exposing yourself."

The pursuit lasted but a little while, and died away in an occasional distant shot.

"They've quit," Davies announced. "It never entered their stupid heads that they could have caught us on Aliso Hill."

"It can't be done," was Charley Drexel's quick judgment of youth, as the machine stopped and they surveyed the acute-angled turn on the stiff up-grade of Aliso. Beneath was the swift-running river.

"Get out everybody!" Wemple commanded. "Up-side, all of you, if you don't want the car to turn over on you. Spread traction wherever she needs it."

"Shoot her ahead, or back—she can't stop," Davies said quietly, from the outer edge of the road, where he had taken position. "The earth's crumbling away from under the tires every second she stands still."

"Get out from under, or she'll be on top of you," Wemple ordered, as he went ahead several yards.

But again, after the car rested a minute, the light, dry earth began to crack and crumble away from under the tires, rolling in a miniature avalanche down the steep declivity into the water. And not until Wemple had backed fifty yards down the narrow road did he find solid resting for the car. He came ahead on foot and examined the acute angle formed by the two zig-zags. Together with Davies he planned what was to be done.

"When you come you've got to come a-humping," Davies advised. "If you stop anywhere for more than seconds, it's good night, and the walking won't be fine."

"She's full of fight, and she can do it. See that hard formation right there on the inside wall. It couldn't have come at a better spot. If I don't make her hind wheels climb half way up it, we'll start walking about a second thereafter."

"She's a two-fisted piece of machinery," Davies encouraged. "I know her kind. If she can't do it, no machine can that was ever made. Am I right, Beth?"

"She's a regular, spunky she-devil," Miss Drexel laughed agreement. "And so are the pair of you—er—of the male persuasion, I mean."

Miss Drexel had never seemed so fascinating to either of them as she was then, in the excitement quite unconscious of her abbreviated costume, her brown hair flying, her eyes sparkling, her lips smiling. Each man caught the other in that moment's pause to look, and each man sighed to the other and looked frankly into each other's eyes ere he turned to the work at hand.

Wemple came up with his usual rush, but it was a gauged rush; and Davies took the post of danger, the outside running board, where his weight would help the broad tires to bite a little deeper into the treacherous surface. If the road-edge crumbled away it was inevitable that he would be caught under the car as it rolled over and down to the river.

It was ahead and reverse, ahead and reverse, with only the briefest of pauses in which to shift the gears. Wemple backed up the hard formation on the inside bank till the car seemed standing on end, rushed ahead till the earth of the outer edge broke under the front tires and splashed in the water. Davies, now off, and again on the running board when needed, accompanied the car in its jerky and erratic progress, tossing robes and coats under the tires, calling instructions to Drexel similarly occupied on the other side, and warning Miss Drexel out of the way.

"Oh, you Merry Olds, you Merry Olds, you Merry Olds," Wemple muttered aloud, as if in prayer, as he wrestled the car about the narrow area, gaining sometimes inches in pivoting it, sometimes fetching back up the inner wall precisely at the spot previously attained, and, once, having the car, with the surface of the roadbed under it, slide bodily and sidewise, two feet down the road.

The clapping of Miss Drexel's hands was the first warning Davies received that the feat was accomplished, and, swinging on to the running board, he found the car backing in the straight-away up the next zig-zag and Wemple still chanting ecstatically, "Oh, you Merry Olds, you Merry Olds!"

There were no more grades nor zigzags between them and Tampico, but, so narrow was the primitive road, two miles farther were backed before space was found in which to turn around. One thing of importance did lie between them and Tampico—namely the investing lines of the constitutionalists. But here, at noon, fortune favored in the form of three American soldiers of fortune, operators of machine guns, who had fought the entire campaign with Villa from the beginning of the advance from the Texan border. Under a white flag, Wemple drove the car across the zone of debate into the federal lines, where good fortune, in the guise of an ubiquitous German naval officer, again received them.

"I think you are nearly the only Americans left in Tampico," he told them. "About all the rest are lying out in the Gulf on the different warships. But at the Southern Hotel there are several, and the situation seems quieter."

As they got out at the Southern, Davies laid his hand on the car and murmured, "Good old girl!" Wemple followed suit. And Miss Drexel, engaging both men's eyes and about to say something, was guilty of a sudden moisture in her own eyes that made her turn to the car with a caressing hand

and repeat, "Good old girl!"

About Author

Family

Jack London's mother, Flora Wellman, was the fifth and youngest child of Pennsylvania Canal builder Marshall Wellman and his first wife, Eleanor Garrett Jones. Marshall Wellman was descended from Thomas Wellman, an early Puritan settler in the Massachusetts Bay Colony. Flora left Ohio and moved to the Pacific coast when her father remarried after her mother died. In San Francisco, Flora worked as a music teacher and spiritualist, claiming to channel the spirit of a Sauk chief, Black Hawk.

Biographer Clarice Stasz and others believe London's father was astrologer William Chaney. Flora Wellman was living with Chaney in San Francisco when she became pregnant. Whether Wellman and Chaney were legally married is unknown. Most San Francisco civil records were destroyed by the extensive fires that followed the 1906 earthquake; nobody knows what name appeared on her son's birth certificate. Stasz notes that in his memoirs, Chaney refers to London's mother Flora Wellman as having been his "wife"; he also cites an advertisement in which Flora called herself "Florence Wellman Chaney".

According to Flora Wellman's account, as recorded in the San Francisco Chronicle of June 4, 1875, Chaney demanded that she have an abortion. When she refused, he disclaimed responsibility for the child. In desperation, she shot herself. She was not seriously wounded, but she was temporarily deranged. After giving birth, Flora turned the baby over for care to Virginia Prentiss, an African-American woman and former slave. She was a major maternal figure throughout London's life. Late in 1876, Flora Wellman married John London, a partially disabled Civil War veteran, and brought her baby John, later known as Jack, to live with the newly married couple. The family moved around the San Francisco Bay Area before settling in Oakland, where London completed public grade school.

In 1897, when he was 21 and a student at the University of California,

Berkeley, London searched for and read the newspaper accounts of his mother's suicide attempt and the name of his biological father. He wrote to William Chaney, then living in Chicago. Chaney responded that he could not be London's father because he was impotent; he casually asserted that London's mother had relations with other men and averred that she had slandered him when she said he insisted on an abortion. Chaney concluded by saying that he was more to be pitied than London. London was devastated by his father's letter; in the months following, he quit school at Berkeley and went to the Klondike during the gold rush boom.

Early life

London was born near Third and Brannan Streets in San Francisco. The house burned down in the fire after the 1906 San Francisco earthquake; the California Historical Society placed a plaque at the site in 1953. Although the family was working class, it was not as impoverished as London's later accounts claimed. London was largely self-educated.

In 1885, London found and read Ouida's long Victorian novel Signa. He credited this as the seed of his literary success. In 1886, he went to the Oakland Public Library and found a sympathetic librarian, Ina Coolbrith, who encouraged his learning. (She later became California's first poet laureate and an important figure in the San Francisco literary community).

In 1889, London began working 12 to 18 hours a day at Hickmott's Cannery. Seeking a way out, he borrowed money from his foster mother Virginia Prentiss, bought the sloop Razzle-Dazzle from an oyster pirate named French Frank, and became an oyster pirate himself. In his memoir, John Barleycorn, he claims also to have stolen French Frank's mistress Mamie. After a few months, his sloop became damaged beyond repair. London hired on as a member of the California Fish Patrol.

In 1893, he signed on to the sealing schooner Sophie Sutherland, bound for the coast of Japan. When he returned, the country was in the grip of the panic of '93 and Oakland was swept by labor unrest. After grueling jobs in a jute mill and a street-railway power plant, London joined Coxey's Army and began his career as a tramp. In 1894, he spent 30 days for vagrancy in the Erie County Penitentiary at Buffalo, New York. In The Road, he wrote:

Man-handling was merely one of the very minor unprintable horrors of the Erie County Pen. I say 'unprintable'; and in justice I must also say undescribable. They were unthinkable to me until I saw them, and I was no spring chicken in the ways of the world and the awful abysses of human degradation. It would take a deep plummet to reach bottom in the Erie County Pen, and I do but skim lightly and facetiously the surface of things as I there saw them.

After many experiences as a hobo and a sailor, he returned to Oakland and attended Oakland High School. He contributed a number of articles to the high school's magazine, The Aegis. His first published work was "Typhoon off the Coast of Japan", an account of his sailing experiences.

As a schoolboy, London often studied at Heinold's First and Last Chance Saloon, a port-side bar in Oakland. At 17, he confessed to the bar's owner, John Heinold, his desire to attend university and pursue a career as a writer. Heinold lent London tuition money to attend college.

London desperately wanted to attend the University of California, Berkeley. In 1896, after a summer of intense studying to pass certification exams, he was admitted. Financial circumstances forced him to leave in 1897 and he never graduated. No evidence suggests that London wrote for student publications while studying at Berkeley.

While at Berkeley, London continued to study and spend time at Heinold's saloon, where he was introduced to the sailors and adventurers who would influence his writing. In his autobiographical novel, John Barleycorn, London mentioned the pub's likeness seventeen times. Heinold's was the place where London met Alexander McLean, a captain known for his cruelty at sea. London based his protagonist Wolf Larsen, in the novel The Sea-Wolf, on McLean.

Heinold's First and Last Chance Saloon is now unofficially named Jack London's Rendezvous in his honor.

Gold rush and first success

On July 12, 1897, London (age 21) and his sister's husband Captain Shepard sailed to join the Klondike Gold Rush. This was the setting for some of his first successful stories. London's time in the harsh Klondike, however, was detrimental to his health. Like so many other men who were malnourished in the goldfields, London developed scurvy. His gums became swollen, leading to the loss of his four front teeth. A constant gnawing pain affected his hip and leg muscles, and his face was stricken with marks that always reminded him of the struggles he faced in the Klondike. Father William Judge, "The Saint of Dawson", had a facility in Dawson that provided shelter, food and any available medicine to London and others. His struggles there inspired London's short story, "To Build a Fire" (1902, revised in 1908), which many critics assess as his best.

His landlords in Dawson were mining engineers Marshall Latham Bond and Louis Whitford Bond, educated at Yale and Stanford, respectively. The brothers' father, Judge Hiram Bond, was a wealthy mining investor. The Bonds, especially Hiram, were active Republicans. Marshall Bond's diary mentions friendly sparring with London on political issues as a camp pastime.

London left Oakland with a social conscience and socialist leanings; he returned to become an activist for socialism. He concluded that his only hope of escaping the work "trap" was to get an education and "sell his brains". He saw his writing as a business, his ticket out of poverty, and, he hoped, a means of beating the wealthy at their own game. On returning to California in 1898, London began working to get published, a struggle described in his novel, Martin Eden (serialized in 1908, published in 1909). His first published story since high school was "To the Man On Trail", which has frequently been collected in anthologies. When The Overland Monthly offered him only five dollars for it—and was slow paying—London came close to abandoning his writing career. In his words, "literally and literarily I was saved" when The Black Cat accepted his story "A Thousand Deaths", and paid him $40—the "first money I ever received for a story".

London began his writing career just as new printing technologies enabled lower-cost production of magazines. This resulted in a boom in popular magazines aimed at a wide public audience and a strong market for short fiction. In 1900, he made $2,500 in writing, about $75,000 in today's currency. Among the works he sold to magazines was a short story known as either "Diable" (1902) or "Bâtard" (1904), two editions of the same basic story; London received $141.25 for this story on May 27, 1902. In the text, a cruel French Canadian brutalizes his dog, and the dog retaliates and kills the man. London told some of his critics that man's actions are the main cause of the behavior of their animals, and he would show this in another story, The Call of the Wild.

In early 1903, London sold The Call of the Wild to The Saturday Evening Post for $750, and the book rights to Macmillan for $2,000. Macmillan's promotional campaign propelled it to swift success.

While living at his rented villa on Lake Merritt in Oakland, California, London met poet George Sterling; in time they became best friends. In 1902, Sterling helped London find a home closer to his own in nearby Piedmont. In his letters London addressed Sterling as "Greek", owing to Sterling's aquiline nose and classical profile, and he signed them as "Wolf". London was later to depict Sterling as Russ Brissenden in his autobiographical novel Martin Eden (1910) and as Mark Hall in The Valley of the Moon (1913).

In later life London indulged his wide-ranging interests by accumulating a personal library of 15,000 volumes. He referred to his books as "the tools of my trade".

First marriage (1900–04)

London married Elizabeth "Bessie" Maddern on April 7, 1900, the same day The Son of the Wolf was published. Bess had been part of his circle of friends for a number of years. She was related to stage actresses Minnie Maddern Fiske and Emily Stevens. Stasz says, "Both acknowledged publicly that they were not marrying out of love, but from friendship and a belief that they would produce sturdy children." Kingman says, "they were comfortable together... Jack had made it clear to Bessie that he did not love her, but that he liked her enough to make a successful marriage."

London met Bessie through his friend at Oakland High School, Fred Jacobs; she was Fred's fiancee. Bessie, who tutored at Anderson's University Academy in Alameda California, tutored Jack in preparation for his entrance exams for the University of California at Berkeley in 1896. Jacobs was killed aboard the USAT Scandia in 1897, but Jack and Bessie continued their friendship, which included taking photos and developing the film together. This was the beginning of Jack's passion for photography.

During the marriage, London continued his friendship with Anna Strunsky, co-authoring The Kempton-Wace Letters, an epistolary novel contrasting two philosophies of love. Anna, writing "Dane Kempton's" letters, arguing for a romantic view of marriage, while London, writing "Herbert Wace's" letters, argued for a scientific view, based on Darwinism and eugenics. In the novel, his fictional character contrasted two women he had known.

London's pet name for Bess was "Mother-Girl" and Bess's for London was "Daddy-Boy". Their first child, Joan, was born on January 15, 1901, and their second, Bessie (later called Becky), on October 20, 1902. Both children were born in Piedmont, California. Here London wrote one of his most celebrated works, The Call of the Wild.

While London had pride in his children, the marriage was strained. Kingman says that by 1903 the couple were close to separation as they were "extremely incompatible". "Jack was still so kind and gentle with Bessie that when Cloudsley Johns was a house guest in February 1903 he didn't suspect a breakup of their marriage."

London reportedly complained to friends Joseph Noel and George Sterling:

[Bessie] is devoted to purity. When I tell her morality is only evidence of low blood pressure, she hates me. She'd sell me and the children out for her damned purity. It's terrible. Every time I come back after being away from home for a night she won't let me be in the same room with her if she can help it.

Stasz writes that these were "code words for [Bess's] fear that [Jack] was consorting with prostitutes and might bring home venereal disease."

On July 24, 1903, London told Bessie he was leaving and moved out. During 1904, London and Bess negotiated the terms of a divorce, and the decree was granted on November 11, 1904.

War correspondent (1904)

London accepted an assignment of the San Francisco Examiner to cover the Russo-Japanese War in early 1904, arriving in Yokohama on January 25, 1904. He was arrested by Japanese authorities in Shimonoseki, but released through the intervention of American ambassador Lloyd Griscom. After travelling to Korea, he was again arrested by Japanese authorities for straying too close to the border with Manchuria without official permission, and was sent back to Seoul. Released again, London was permitted to travel with the Imperial Japanese Army to the border, and to observe the Battle of the Yalu.

London asked William Randolph Hearst, the owner of the San Francisco Examiner, to be allowed to transfer to the Imperial Russian Army, where he felt that restrictions on his reporting and his movements would be less severe. However, before this could be arranged, he was arrested for a third time in four months, this time for assaulting his Japanese assistants, whom he accused of stealing the fodder for his horse. Released through the personal intervention of President Theodore Roosevelt, London departed the front in June 1904.

Bohemian Club

On August 18, 1904, London went with his close friend, the poet George Sterling, to "Summer High Jinks" at the Bohemian Grove. London was elected to honorary membership in the Bohemian Club and took part in many activities. Other noted members of the Bohemian Club during this time included Ambrose Bierce, Gelett Burgess, Allan Dunn, John Muir, Frank Norris, and Herman George Scheffauer.

Beginning in December 1914, London worked on The Acorn Planter, A California Forest Play, to be performed as one of the annual Grove Plays, but it was never selected. It was described as too difficult to set to music. London published The Acorn Planter in 1916.

Second marriage

After divorcing Maddern, London married Charmian Kittredge in 1905. London was introduced to Kittredge in 1900 by her aunt Netta Eames, who was an editor at Overland Monthly magazine in San Francisco. The two met prior to his first marriage but became lovers years later after Jack and Bessie London visited Wake Robin, Netta Eames' Sonoma County resort, in 1903. London was injured when he fell from a buggy, and Netta arranged for Charmian to care for him. The two developed a friendship, as Charmian, Netta, her husband Roscoe, and London were politically aligned with socialist causes. At some point the relationship became romantic, and Jack divorced his wife to marry Charmian, who was five years his senior.

Biographer Russ Kingman called Charmian "Jack's soul-mate, always at his side, and a perfect match." Their time together included numerous trips, including a 1907 cruise on the yacht Snark to Hawaii and Australia. Many of London's stories are based on his visits to Hawaii, the last one for 10 months beginning in December 1915.

The couple also visited Goldfield, Nevada, in 1907, where they were guests of the Bond brothers, London's Dawson City landlords. The Bond brothers were working in Nevada as mining engineers.

London had contrasted the concepts of the "Mother Girl" and the "Mate Woman" in The Kempton-Wace Letters. His pet name for Bess had been "Mother-Girl;" his pet name for Charmian was "Mate-Woman." Charmian's aunt and foster mother, a disciple of Victoria Woodhull, had raised her without prudishness. Every biographer alludes to Charmian's uninhibited sexuality.

Joseph Noel calls the events from 1903 to 1905 "a domestic drama that would have intrigued the pen of an Ibsen.... London's had comedy relief in it

112

and a sort of easy-going romance." In broad outline, London was restless in his first marriage, sought extramarital sexual affairs, and found, in Charmian Kittredge, not only a sexually active and adventurous partner, but his future life-companion. They attempted to have children; one child died at birth, and another pregnancy ended in a miscarriage.

In 1906, London published in Collier's magazine his eye-witness report of the San Francisco earthquake.

Beauty Ranch (1905–16)

In 1905, London purchased a 1,000 acres (4.0 km2) ranch in Glen Ellen, Sonoma County, California, on the eastern slope of Sonoma Mountain, for $26,450. He wrote: "Next to my wife, the ranch is the dearest thing in the world to me." He desperately wanted the ranch to become a successful business enterprise. Writing, always a commercial enterprise with London, now became even more a means to an end: "I write for no other purpose than to add to the beauty that now belongs to me. I write a book for no other reason than to add three or four hundred acres to my magnificent estate."

Stasz writes that London "had taken fully to heart the vision, expressed in his agrarian fiction, of the land as the closest earthly version of Eden ... he educated himself through the study of agricultural manuals and scientific tomes. He conceived of a system of ranching that today would be praised for its ecological wisdom." He was proud to own the first concrete silo in California, a circular piggery that he designed. He hoped to adapt the wisdom of Asian sustainable agriculture to the United States. He hired both Italian and Chinese stonemasons, whose distinctly different styles are obvious.

The ranch was an economic failure. Sympathetic observers such as Stasz treat his projects as potentially feasible, and ascribe their failure to bad luck or to being ahead of their time. Unsympathetic historians such as Kevin Starr suggest that he was a bad manager, distracted by other concerns and impaired by his alcoholism. Starr notes that London was absent from his ranch about six months a year between 1910 and 1916 and says, "He liked the show of managerial power, but not grinding attention to detail .... London's workers laughed at his efforts to play big-time rancher [and considered] the operation a rich man's hobby."

London spent $80,000 ($2,230,000 in current value) to build a 15,000-square-foot (1,400 m2) stone mansion called Wolf House on the property. Just as the mansion was nearing completion, two weeks before the Londons planned to move in, it was destroyed by fire.

London's last visit to Hawaii, beginning in December 1915, lasted eight months. He met with Duke Kahanamoku, Prince Jonah Kūhiō Kalaniana'ole, Queen Lili'uokalani and many others, before returning to his ranch in July 1916. He was suffering from kidney failure, but he continued to work.

The ranch (abutting stone remnants of Wolf House) is now a National Historic Landmark and is protected in Jack London State Historic Park.

Animal activism

London witnessed animal cruelty in the training of circus animals, and his subsequent novels Jerry of the Islands and Michael, Brother of Jerry included a foreword entreating the public to become more informed about this practice. In 1918, the Massachusetts Society for the Prevention of Cruelty to Animals and the American Humane Education Society teamed up to create the Jack London Club, which sought to inform the public about cruelty to circus animals and encourage them to protest this establishment. Support from Club members led to a temporary cessation of trained animal acts at Ringling-Barnum and Bailey in 1925.

Death

London died November 22, 1916, in a sleeping porch in a cottage on his ranch. London had been a robust man but had suffered several serious illnesses, including scurvy in the Klondike. Additionally, during travels on the Snark, he and Charmian picked up unspecified tropical infections, and diseases, including yaws. At the time of his death, he suffered from dysentery, late-stage alcoholism, and uremia; he was in extreme pain and taking morphine.

London's ashes were buried on his property not far from the Wolf House. London's funeral took place on November 26, 1916, attended only by close friends, relatives, and workers of the property. In accordance with his wishes, he was cremated and buried next to some pioneer children, under a rock that belonged to the Wolf House. After Charmian's death in 1955, she was also cremated and then buried with her husband in the same simple spot that her husband chose. The grave is marked by a mossy boulder. The buildings and property were later preserved as Jack London State Historic Park, in Glen Ellen, California.

Suicide debate

Because he was using morphine, many older sources describe London's death as a suicide, and some still do. This conjecture appears to be a rumor, or speculation based on incidents in his fiction writings. His death certificate gives the cause as uremia, following acute renal colic.

The biographer Stasz writes, "Following London's death, for a number of reasons, a biographical myth developed in which he has been portrayed as an alcoholic womanizer who committed suicide. Recent scholarship based upon firsthand documents challenges this caricature." Most biographers, including Russ Kingman, now agree he died of uremia aggravated by an accidental morphine overdose.

London's fiction featured several suicides. In his autobiographical memoir John Barleycorn, he claims, as a youth, to have drunkenly stumbled overboard into the San Francisco Bay, "some maundering fancy of going out with the tide suddenly obsessed me". He said he drifted and nearly succeeded in drowning before sobering up and being rescued by fishermen. In the dénouement of The Little Lady of the Big House, the heroine, confronted by the pain of a mortal gunshot wound, undergoes a physician-assisted suicide by morphine. Also, in Martin Eden, the principal protagonist, who shares certain characteristics with London, drowns himself.

Accusations of plagiarism

London was vulnerable to accusations of plagiarism, both because he was such a conspicuous, prolific, and successful writer and because of his methods of working. He wrote in a letter to Elwyn Hoffman, "expression, you see—with me—is far easier than invention." He purchased plots and novels from the young Sinclair Lewis and used incidents from newspaper clippings as writing material.

In July 1901, two pieces of fiction appeared within the same month: London's "Moon-Face", in the San Francisco Argonaut, and Frank Norris' "The Passing of Cock-eye Blacklock", in Century Magazine. Newspapers showed the similarities between the stories, which London said were "quite different in manner of treatment, [but] patently the same in foundation and motive." London explained both writers based their stories on the same newspaper account. A year later, it was discovered that Charles Forrest McLean had published a fictional story also based on the same incident.

Egerton Ryerson Young claimed The Call of the Wild (1903) was taken from Young's book My Dogs in the Northland (1902). London acknowledged using it as a source and claimed to have written a letter to Young thanking him.

In 1906, the New York World published "deadly parallel" columns showing eighteen passages from London's short story "Love of Life" side by side with similar passages from a nonfiction article by Augustus Biddle and J. K. Macdonald, titled "Lost in the Land of the Midnight Sun". London noted the World did not accuse him of "plagiarism", but only of "identity of time and situation", to which he defiantly "pled guilty".

The most serious charge of plagiarism was based on London's "The Bishop's Vision", Chapter 7 of his novel The Iron Heel (1908). The chapter is nearly identical to an ironic essay that Frank Harris published in 1901, titled "The Bishop of London and Public Morality". Harris was incensed and suggested he should receive 1/60th of the royalties from The Iron Heel, the disputed material constituting about that fraction of the whole novel. London insisted he had clipped a reprint of the article, which had appeared in an American newspaper, and believed it to be a genuine speech delivered by the Bishop of London.

Views

Atheism

London was an atheist. He is quoted as saying, "I believe that when I am dead, I am dead. I believe that with my death I am just as much obliterated as the last mosquito you and I squashed."

Socialism

London wrote from a socialist viewpoint, which is evident in his novel The Iron Heel. Neither a theorist nor an intellectual socialist, London's socialism grew out of his life experience. As London explained in his essay, "How I Became a Socialist", his views were influenced by his experience with people at the bottom of the social pit. His optimism and individualism faded, and he vowed never to do more hard physical work than necessary. He wrote that his individualism was hammered out of him, and he was politically reborn. He often closed his letters "Yours for the Revolution."

London joined the Socialist Labor Party in April 1896. In the same year, the San Francisco Chronicle published a story about the twenty-year-old London's giving nightly speeches in Oakland's City Hall Park, an activity he was arrested for a year later. In 1901, he left the Socialist Labor Party and joined the new Socialist Party of America. He ran unsuccessfully as the high-profile Socialist candidate for mayor of Oakland in 1901 (receiving 245 votes) and 1905 (improving to 981 votes), toured the country lecturing on socialism in 1906, and published two collections of essays about socialism: The War of the Classes (1905) and Revolution, and other Essays (1906).

Stasz notes that "London regarded the Wobblies as a welcome addition to the Socialist cause, although he never joined them in going so far as to recommend sabotage." Stasz mentions a personal meeting between London and Big Bill Haywood in 1912.

In his late (1913) book The Cruise of the Snark, London writes about appeals to him for membership of the Snark's crew from office workers and other "toilers" who longed for escape from the cities, and of being cheated by workmen.

In his Glen Ellen ranch years, London felt some ambivalence toward socialism and complained about the "inefficient Italian labourers" in his employ. In 1916, he resigned from the Glen Ellen chapter of the Socialist Party, but stated emphatically he did so "because of its lack of fire and fight, and its loss of emphasis on the class struggle." In an unflattering portrait of London's ranch days, California cultural historian Kevin Starr refers to this period as "post-socialist" and says "... by 1911 ... London was more bored by the class struggle than he cared to admit."

Racial views

London shared common concerns among European Americans in California about Asian immigration, described as "the yellow peril"; he used the latter term as the title of a 1904 essay. This theme was also the subject of a story he wrote in 1910 called "The Unparalleled Invasion". Presented as an historical essay set in the future, the story narrates events between 1976 and 1987, in which China, with an ever-increasing population, is taking over and colonizing its neighbors with the intention of taking over the entire Earth. The western nations respond with biological warfare and bombard China with dozens of the most infectious diseases. On his fears about China, he admits, "it must be taken into consideration that the above postulate is itself a product of Western race-egotism, urged by our belief in our own righteousness and fostered by a faith in ourselves which may be as erroneous as are most fond race fancies."

By contrast, many of London's short stories are notable for their empathetic portrayal of Mexican ("The Mexican"), Asian ("The Chinago"), and Hawaiian ("Koolau the Leper") characters. London's war correspondence from the Russo-Japanese War, as well as his unfinished novel Cherry, show he admired much about Japanese customs and capabilities. London's writings have been popular among the Japanese, who believe he portrayed them positively.

In "Koolau the Leper", London describes Koolau, who is a Hawaiian leper—and thus a very different sort of "superman" than Martin Eden—and who fights off an entire cavalry troop to elude capture, as "indomitable spiritually—a ... magnificent rebel". This character is based on Hawaiian leper Kaluaikoolau, who in 1893 revolted and resisted capture from forces of the Provisional Government of Hawaii in the Kalalau Valley.

An amateur boxer and avid boxing fan, London reported on the 1910 Johnson–Jeffries fight, in which the black boxer Jack Johnson vanquished Jim Jeffries, known as the "Great White Hope". In 1908, London had reported on an earlier fight of Johnson's, contrasting the black boxer's coolness and intellectual style, with the apelike appearance and fighting style of his Canadian opponent, Tommy Burns,

'what . . . [won] on Saturday was bigness, coolness, quickness, cleverness, and vast physical superiority... Because a white man wishes a white man to win, this should not prevent him from giving absolute credit to the best man, even when that best man was black. All hail to Johnson.' London wrote that Johnson was 'superb. He was impregnable . . . as inaccessible as Mont Blanc.'

Those who defend London against charges of racism cite the letter he wrote to the Japanese-American Commercial Weekly in 1913:

In reply to yours of August 16, 1913. First of all, I should say by stopping the stupid newspaper from always fomenting race prejudice. This of course, being impossible, I would say, next, by educating the people of Japan so that they will be too intelligently tolerant to respond to any call to race prejudice. And, finally, by realizing, in industry and government, of socialism—which last word is merely a word that stands for the actual application of in the affairs of men of the theory of the Brotherhood of Man.

In the meantime the nations and races are only unruly boys who have not yet grown to the stature of men. So we must expect them to do unruly and boisterous things at times. And, just as boys grow up, so the races of mankind will grow up and laugh when they look back upon their childish quarrels.

In 1996, after the City of Whitehorse, Yukon, renamed a street in honor of London, protests over London's alleged racism forced the city to change the name of "Jack London Boulevard" back to "Two-mile Hill".

Works

Short stories

Western writer and historian Dale L. Walker writes:

London's true métier was the short story ... London's true genius lay in the short form, 7,500 words and under, where the flood of images in his teeming brain and the innate power of his narrative gift were at once constrained and freed. His stories that run longer than the magic 7,500 generally—but certainly not always—could have benefited from self-editing.

London's "strength of utterance" is at its height in his stories, and they are painstakingly well-constructed. "To Build a Fire" is the best known of all his stories. Set in the harsh Klondike, it recounts the haphazard trek of a new arrival who has ignored an old-timer's warning about the risks of traveling alone. Falling through the ice into a creek in seventy-five-below weather, the unnamed man is keenly aware that survival depends on his untested skills at quickly building a fire to dry his clothes and warm his extremities. After publishing a tame version of this story—with a sunny outcome—in The Youth's Companion in 1902, London offered a second, more severe take on the man's predicament in The Century Magazine in 1908. Reading both provides an illustration of London's growth and maturation as a writer. As Labor (1994) observes: "To compare the two versions is itself an instructive lesson in what distinguished a great work of literary art from a good children's story."

Other stories from the Klondike period include: "All Gold Canyon", about a battle between a gold prospector and a claim jumper; "The Law of Life", about an aging American Indian man abandoned by his tribe and left to die; "Love of Life", about a trek by a prospector across the Canadian tundra; "To the Man on Trail," which tells the story of a prospector fleeing the Mounted Police in a sled race, and raises the question of the contrast between written law and morality; and "An Odyssey of the North," which

120

raises questions of conditional morality, and paints a sympathetic portrait of a man of mixed White and Aleut ancestry.

London was a boxing fan and an avid amateur boxer. "A Piece of Steak" is a tale about a match between older and younger boxers. It contrasts the differing experiences of youth and age but also raises the social question of the treatment of aging workers. "The Mexican" combines boxing with a social theme, as a young Mexican endures an unfair fight and ethnic prejudice in order to earn money with which to aid the revolution.

Several of London's stories would today be classified as science fiction. "The Unparalleled Invasion" describes germ warfare against China; "Goliath" is about an irresistible energy weapon; "The Shadow and the Flash" is a tale about two brothers who take different routes to achieving invisibility; "A Relic of the Pliocene" is a tall tale about an encounter of a modern-day man with a mammoth. "The Red One" is a late story from a period when London was intrigued by the theories of the psychiatrist and writer Jung. It tells of an island tribe held in thrall by an extraterrestrial object.

Some nineteen original collections of short stories were published during London's brief life or shortly after his death. There have been several posthumous anthologies drawn from this pool of stories. Many of these stories were located in the Klondike and the Pacific. A collection of Jack London's San Francisco Stories was published in October 2010 by Sydney Samizdat Press.

Novels

London's most famous novels are The Call of the Wild, White Fang, The Sea-Wolf, The Iron Heel, and Martin Eden.

In a letter dated Dec 27, 1901, London's Macmillan publisher George Platt Brett, Sr., said "he believed Jack's fiction represented 'the very best kind of work' done in America."

Critic Maxwell Geismar called The Call of the Wild "a beautiful prose poem"; editor Franklin Walker said that it "belongs on a shelf with Walden and Huckleberry Finn"; and novelist E.L. Doctorow called it "a mordant parable ... his masterpiece."

The historian Dale L. Walker commented:

Jack London was an uncomfortable novelist, that form too long for his natural impatience and the quickness of his mind. His novels, even the best of them, are hugely flawed.

Some critics have said that his novels are episodic and resemble linked short stories. Dale L. Walker writes:

The Star Rover, that magnificent experiment, is actually a series of short stories connected by a unifying device ... Smoke Bellew is a series of stories bound together in a novel-like form by their reappearing protagonist, Kit Bellew; and John Barleycorn ... is a synoptic series of short episodes.

Ambrose Bierce said of The Sea-Wolf that "the great thing—and it is among the greatest of things—is that tremendous creation, Wolf Larsen ... the hewing out and setting up of such a figure is enough for a man to do in one lifetime." However, he noted, "The love element, with its absurd suppressions, and impossible proprieties, is awful."

The Iron Heel is interesting as an example of a dystopian novel that anticipates and influenced George Orwell's Nineteen Eighty-Four. London's socialist politics are explicitly on display here. The Iron Heel meets the contemporary definition of soft science fiction. The Star Rover (1915) is also science fiction.

Apocrypha

Jack London Credo

London's literary executor, Irving Shepard, quoted a Jack London Credo in an introduction to a 1956 collection of London stories:

I would rather be ashes than dust!

I would rather that my spark should burn out in a brilliant blaze than it should be stifled by dry-rot.

I would rather be a superb meteor, every atom of me in magnificent glow, than a sleepy and permanent planet.

The function of man is to live, not to exist.

I shall not waste my days in trying to prolong them.

I shall use my time.

The biographer Stasz notes that the passage "has many marks of London's style" but the only line that could be safely attributed to London was the first. The words Shepard quoted were from a story in the San Francisco Bulletin, December 2, 1916, by journalist Ernest J. Hopkins, who visited the ranch just weeks before London's death. Stasz notes, "Even more so than today journalists' quotes were unreliable or even sheer inventions," and says no direct source in London's writings has been found. However, at least one line, according to Stasz, is authentic, being referenced by London and written in his own hand in the autograph book of Australian suffragette Vida Goldstein:

Dear Miss Goldstein:–

Seven years ago I wrote you that I'd rather be ashes than dust. I still subscribe to that sentiment.

Sincerely yours,

Jack London

Jan. 13, 1909

Furthermore, in his short story "By The Turtles of Tasman", a character, defending her ne'er-do-well grasshopperish father to her antlike uncle, says: "... my father has been a king. He has lived .... Have you lived merely to live? Are you afraid to die? I'd rather sing one wild song and burst my heart with it, than live a thousand years watching my digestion and being afraid of the wet. When you are dust, my father will be ashes."

"The Scab"

A short diatribe on "The Scab" is often quoted within the U.S. labor movement and frequently attributed to London. It opens:

After God had finished the rattlesnake, the toad, and the vampire, he had some awful substance left with which he made a scab. A scab is a two-legged animal with a corkscrew soul, a water brain, a combination backbone of jelly and glue. Where others have hearts, he carries a tumor of rotten principles. When a scab comes down the street, men turn their backs and Angels weep in Heaven, and the Devil shuts the gates of hell to keep him out....

In 1913 and 1914, a number of newspapers printed the first three sentences with varying terms used instead of "scab", such as "knocker", "stool pigeon" or "scandal monger".

This passage as given above was the subject of a 1974 Supreme Court case, Letter Carriers v. Austin, in which Justice Thurgood Marshall referred to it as "a well-known piece of trade union literature, generally attributed to author Jack London". A union newsletter had published a "list of scabs," which was granted to be factual and therefore not libelous, but then went on to quote the passage as the "definition of a scab". The case turned on the question of whether the "definition" was defamatory. The court ruled that "Jack London's... 'definition of a scab' is merely rhetorical hyperbole, a lusty and imaginative expression of the contempt felt by union members towards those who refuse to join", and as such was not libelous and was protected under the First Amendment.

Despite being frequently attributed to London, the passage does not appear at all in the extensive collection of his writings at Sonoma State University's website. However, in his book The War of the Classes he published a 1903 speech entitled "The Scab", which gave a much more balanced view of the topic:

The laborer who gives more time or strength or skill for the same wage than another, or equal time or strength or skill for a less wage, is a scab. The generousness on his part is hurtful to his fellow-laborers, for it compels them to an equal generousness which is not to their liking, and which gives them less of food and shelter. But a word may be said for the scab. Just as his act makes his rivals compulsorily generous, so do they, by fortune of birth and training, make compulsory his act of generousness.

[...]

Nobody desires to scab, to give most for least. The ambition of every individual is quite the opposite, to give least for most; and, as a result, living in a tooth-and-nail society, battle royal is waged by the ambitious individuals. But in its most salient aspect, that of the struggle over the division of the joint product, it is no longer a battle between individuals, but between groups of individuals. Capital and labor apply themselves to raw material, make something useful out of it, add to its value, and then proceed to quarrel over the division of the added value. Neither cares to give most for least. Each is intent on giving less than the other and on receiving more. (Source: Wikipedia)

Printed in July 2019
by Rotomail Italia S.p.A., Vignate (MI) - Italy